**Don't miss these other spellbinding novels by
DONNA GRANT**

Midnight's Temptation
Midnight's Promise
Midnight's Surrender

DARK SWORD SERIES

Dangerous Highlander
Forbidden Highlander
Wicked Highlander
Untamed Highlander
Shadow Highlander
Darkest Highlander

SHIELD SERIES

A Dark Guardian
A Kind of Magic
A Dark Seduction
A Forbidden Temptation
A Warrior's Heart

DRUIDS GLEN SERIES

Highland Mist
Highland Nights
Highland Dawn
Highland Fires
Highland Magic
Dragonfyre

SISTERS OF MAGIC TRILOGY

Shadow Magic
Echoes of Magic
Dangerous Magic

And look for more anticipated novels from Donna Grant

Soul Scorched (Dark Kings)
*Wild Flame (*Chiasson*)*
Moon Struck (LaRue)

coming soon!

MOON THRALL

A LaRue Story

DONNA GRANT

This is a work of fiction. All of the characters, organizations, and events portrayed in this novel are either products of the author's imagination or are used fictitiously.

Moon Thrall
© 2015 by DL Grant, LLC
Excerpt from *Wild Flame* copyright © 2015 by Donna Grant

Cover design © 2014 by Leah Suttle

ISBN 10: 1942017170
ISBN 13: 978- 1942017172

www.DonnaGrant.com

Available in ebook and print editions

PRONUNCIATIONS & GLOSSARY

GLOSSARY:

Andouille (ahn-doo-ee) & **Boudin** (boo-dan)
Two types of Cajun sausage. Andouille is made with pork while boudin with pork and rice.

Bayou (by-you)
A sluggish stream bigger than a creek and smaller than a river

Beignet (bin-yay)
A fritter or doughnut without a hole, sprinkled with powdered sugar

Cajun ('ka-jun)
A person of French-Canadian descent born or living along southern Louisiana.

Etoufee (ay-two-fay)
Tangy tomato-based sauce dish usually made with crawfish or shrimp and rice

Gumbo (gum-bo)
Thick, savory soup with chicken, seafood, sausage, or wild game

Hoodoo (hu-du)
Also known as "conjure" or witchcraft. Thought of as "folk magic" and "superstition". Some say it is the main force against the use of Voodoo.

Jambalaya (jom-bah-LIE-yah)
Highly seasoned mixture of sausage, chicken, or seafood and vegetables, simmered with rice until liquid is absorbed

Maman (muh-mahn)
Term used for grandmother

Parish
A Louisiana state district; equivalent to the word county

Sha (a as in cat)
Term of affection meaning darling, dear, or sweetheart.

Voodoo (vu-du) – New Orleans
Spiritual folkways originating in the Caribbean. New Orleans Voodoo is separate from other forms (Haitian Vodou and southern Hoodoo). New Orleans Voodoo puts emphasis on Voodoo Queens and Voodoo dolls.

Zydeco (zy-dey-coh)
Accordion-based music originating in Louisiana combined with guitar and violin while combing traditional French melodies with Caribbean and blues influences

PRONUNCIATION:

Arcineaux (are-cen-o)

Chiasson (ch-ay-son)

Davena (dav-E-na)

Delia (d-ee-l-ee-uh)

Delphine (d-eh-l-FEEN)

Dumas (dOO-mah-s)

Gilbeaux (g-ih-l-b-oh)

Lafayette (lah-fai-EHt)

LaRue (l-er-OO)

Theriot (terry-O)

ACKNOWLEDGEMENTS

A special thanks goes out to my family who lives in the bayous of Louisiana. Those summers there are some of my best memories. I also need to send a shout-out to my team – Bridgette B, Candace C, Stephanie D, Kelly M, Kristin N, Vanessa R, Shani S. You guys are the bomb. Hats off to my editor, Chelle Olson, and design extraordinaire, Leah Suttle. Thank you all for helping me get this story out.

Lots of thanks and love to my incredible family. Thanks for putting up with my hectic schedule and for knowing when it was time that I got out of the house. And a special hug for my furbabies Lexi, Sheba, Sassy, Tinkerbell, and Diego.

Last but not least, my readers. You have my eternal gratitude for the amazing support you show me and my books. Y'all rock my world. Stay tuned at the end of this story for the first sneak peek of *Wild Flame*, Chiasson book 4 out May 18, 2015. Enjoy!

Xoxo
Donna

CHAPTER ONE

September

It was the smell of bacon frying that pulled him from sleep. Court threw an arm over his eyes to block out the light coming through the row of windows behind him.

"This is beyond anything I've read in years," his brother Kane said.

There was a thud that Court recognized as Kane firmly setting down his mug of coffee. Court released a breath, hoping to fall back asleep quickly. It wasn't going to be easy when Kane was sitting at the table six feet away.

"What now?" Riley asked.

His cousin from Lyons Point had been sharing Kane's apartment for weeks now, and it looked like she had no intention of leaving anytime soon.

"This...well, there's no other way to put it. It's shit," Kane grumbled.

Court sat up and glared at both of them. It was wasted since Riley was focused on cooking and Kane was absorbed in reading the paper.

"It's too damn early in the morning for this," Court said as he rose from the couch and shuffled into the kitchen. He palmed a mug and poured himself some coffee.

Riley chuckled as she munched on a slice of crispy bacon and eyed him. "It's not early for us."

"Perhaps if you got in at a reasonable hour," Kane said as he set the paper down. "Besides, tell me again why you aren't at your place?"

Court took two sips of coffee and let the caffeine settle in his stomach before he replied. "It's not my fault the women won't leave me alone."

"You might try not sleeping with the nut jobs," Riley stated and pulled out the last of the bacon before she dumped eggs into the pan and began to scramble them.

Court frowned as he looked at the food, feeling a little jealous that he had been missing out on such a delicious start to the day. "Do you cook for Kane every morning?"

Kane sat back in his chair. "Sometimes I cook."

Riley shot Kane a smile. Court hadn't been sure anyone could bring Kane out of his funk. He hadn't been the same since the chaos that happened in Lyons Point when he had been cursed and sent after Lincoln's woman. Riley was doing what no one else could.

Kane still wasn't his easygoing self – yet. But he

was getting there. He didn't snap at people as often, and Court even saw his mouth easing into what could almost be considered a smile more and more.

"This," Kane said, pointing to the newspaper, "is stupidity at its finest."

Court leaned back against the counter and scratched his bare chest. Kane read the paper religiously every morning. While everyone else had moved into the modern age and either didn't bother to read the paper at all or read it electronically, Kane was still old school.

Riley dished out eggs onto three plates. She turned to the table with plates in each hand and waited as Kane folded the paper so that the article he'd been reading was on top. She set the plates, bacon, and biscuits on the table and motioned for Court to sit as she gathered utensils and napkins. Court hurried to put on his shirt from the night before.

Riley was the last to take her chair at the round table. Then she looked at Kane and asked, "What did you find?"

"An article on the supernatural in New Orleans."

Court shook his head as he cut open a biscuit and slathered it with butter. "That's nothing new."

"It is when the reporter is going to clubs where the supernatural visit and then writing about it."

Riley choked on her coffee. She wiped her mouth with her napkin, her eyes wide. "Are you serious?"

Court watched Kane nod his head of golden blond hair. "It's just a piece in the paper. No one is going to read that drivel, and even if they do, no one will believe the reporter."

"It's not the article that has me so upset," Kane stated around a mouthful of eggs. "It's that she points out the factions and describes some of the leaders perfectly."

Court waited until he swallowed his bite before he asked, "Who is described?"

Kane leaned over the paper and read, "Though tattooing has always been appreciated in our fair city, there is a faction who likes to tat their heads. These beings should be steered clear of at all costs."

"At least she recognizes that the Djinn are dangerous," Riley said.

"People are going to be heading out to the Viper's Nest and Boudreaux's looking for these tattooed people now."

Court realized that Kane had a point. "How long is the article?"

"Long enough." Kane stabbed the eggs with his fork and held the utensil at his mouth for a bite. "This is her third article. I don't expect it to be her last."

Riley swallowed the last of her biscuit while she held another piece of bacon in her hand. "Perhaps I should go have a talk with her."

"That would be a bad idea." Court pushed his cleared plate away and scooted down in his chair as he leaned back. "If we go to her, she'll know that we know something. I don't want to be mentioned in any of her articles."

Kane's lips twisted in revulsion as he chewed. "Her first articles merely mentioned the supernatural part of the city. It seemed harmless enough until this morning. She's visiting these bars, Court. If she's not careful, she's going to die."

"That's what we're for." Riley smiled when they turned to her. "I say 'we' because I have been helping out."

Court stared at his beautiful cousin. Riley had long black hair and the same blue eyes that all the Chiassons and LaRues had. She was tall, lithe, and had a smile that could make the Devil beg her take over Hell itself.

He understood all too well why his four male cousins in Lyons Point had done everything in their power to keep her away from the monsters they hunted. What Riley's brothers didn't understand, was that she was stubborn and completely immovable when she focused on something she wanted.

There was no way Riley wasn't going to help them, whether it was hunting a rogue vampire or protecting a human getting too close to danger. All the LaRues could do was make sure that Riley never went out alone. One of them was always with her to watch her back.

Because none of them wanted the Chiassons descending on New Orleans if Riley got hurt.

Riley flicked her long hair over her shoulder and held Court's gaze. "I've more than pulled my weight in the weeks I've been here."

"Without a doubt," Court agreed.

"Don't you dare start treating me like my brothers do."

Kane rose and walked behind Riley on the way to get more coffee, tugging on her hair. "We're protective, cousin. Even you can understand that. We know you can hold your own."

Court met Kane's gaze as he turned and tilted the mug to his lips. Kane's blue eyes were intense with meaning. Don't fuck this up, was read loud and clear.

That's when Court realized that Kane needed Riley as much as Riley needed him. Whether the two of them knew it or not, each was the anchor for the other.

Kane because he couldn't forgive himself for what had happened to get him doubly cursed by the nastiest of Voodoo priestesses, Delphine, and Riley because her brothers kept pushing her away.

"Riley's right. If we're going to do this, she needs to come along," Court said. "The reporter might respond better if it comes from another female."

Kane ran a hand through his golden blond hair that now came down to his chin. "I'll do some research on her today. Court, you've got fifteen minutes to get to the bar. It's your turn to open."

"Shit," Court said as he jumped out of the chair and grabbed the shoes he had kicked off when he'd crashed there last night.

He stuffed his feet in his boots, made sure he

had his wallet and cell phone, and then he was out the door.

Riley waited until the door shut behind him before she turned in her chair to look at Kane. "He has no idea about the details of your parents' deaths, does he?"

"None." Kane crossed one ankle over the other, his blue gaze still on the door. "There was much he didn't see or know about while we were growing up because he's the youngest. We wanted it that way."

"Trust me when I say that won't turn out well. I'm the youngest as well as the only girl in my family. Having things kept from me only pisses me off."

Kane's gaze lowered, a wall coming down. "I hear you, but that doesn't make revealing them any easier. Court doesn't carry the troubles that Solomon, Myles, or I do. I like it that way."

"If he keeps moving from woman to woman like he has been, you're going to have a different kind of trouble on your hands," she warned.

"He likes the attention from the females." Kane set down his mug and braced his hands behind him on the counter. "There's nothing wrong with that."

"None at all."

After weeks of living with Kane, Riley could tell he was closing himself off again. It happened frequently. Something would trigger a memory or thought, and he would become detached and reserved.

He opened up to her more and more. Progress

was being made, but it wasn't quick enough for Kane's brothers. Solomon had taken her aside the day she'd arrived in New Orleans and asked her to do what she could for Kane.

Most times, Kane was content letting her ramble on as she often did. His gaze would become distant, and she was sure he never heard her. Yet he always had a comment to make after her stories.

She couldn't imagine what Kane was going through. It was bad enough that the LaRues were cursed generations ago to live as werewolves. Then Kane had to go and piss off Delphine.

Riley liked to call her the Bitch Queen. The Voodoo priestess had it out for the LaRues and the Chiassons, mostly because they were the only ones who had the power to keep her in check.

Delphine had put a curse on Kane to seek out Ava Ledet and kill her. Years before, Jack Ledet had killed a vampire who happened to be Delphine's niece. Delphine had never forgiven him for that.

It was all very complicated. Kane had been unable to stop himself from seeking out Ava, who just happened to be in Lyons Point and near Riley's brothers at the time.

The worst part about it wasn't that the curse sent Kane to kill Ava – which was bad enough - it was that if he did, he would remain in werewolf form forever, forgetting who he was.

Luckily, it was Lincoln who'd found Ava – and fell hard for her. Solomon had then arrived in Lyons Point to help Lincoln keep Ava safe, as well as preventing Kane from completing Delphine's task.

It didn't seem to matter to Kane that he wasn't responsible for going after Ava. In his mind, the blame lay squarely with him. His actions ate at him like acid.

Riley rose and walked to Kane. He was so tortured that she wondered if anyone would ever be able to heal him. Myles said time would heal his brother. Riley wasn't so sure.

Every time she thought Kane was making progress, he would revert. Just like now.

She put her hand on his cheek. "Do you need anything?"

"To forget."

The words were spoken so softly she almost didn't hear them. And they broke her heart.

"Delphine no longer has control over you," Riley reminded him. "You control yourself, Kane."

"What about the next time we have to fight her?" His blue gaze clashed with hers. "And what about us combining forces with the Moonstone wolves and every witch group in the quarter to free Addison and Minka from her spell to gain ultimate power? Do you think she's going to let that go?"

Riley tried not to think about what Delphine might do. Everyone knew she would retaliate. It was the when that kept them on edge.

"She won't," Kane continued. "She'll come for one of us. She's more powerful than you can possibly imagine. I fought her spell. I fought with everything I had. Only to lose."

"You won."

Kane shoved her hand away and walked off a few steps then whirled around. "No one wins against that bitch. She keeps score, Riley. She marked us, and she marked your brothers. Do you think you can remain in this city without her turning her attention to you? It'll happen, cousin. If it hasn't already."

"It'll happen no matter where I am," she stated.

But there was no denying the fear that began to spread within her.

CHAPTER TWO

Skye Parrish stood on the sidewalk and smiled as she read over her article on her iPad. Every time she saw her name in print, she realized she was living a dream.

It had taken all her skills to sell herself, and her idea for the articles, to her editor. Helen was a tough bird, but Skye eventually wore her down. Now that her column was gaining more readers each week, Skye couldn't wait to tell everyone what was truly out in the world.

People had a right to know what was living next door to them and who was truly dangerous. Or maybe she should say what. She didn't exactly think the supernatural beings were human. How could they be if they were immortal and had magic?

Skye looked over the so-called fortune tellers in

Jackson Square. They were, in fact, witches. The witch faction in New Orleans was huge. It could easily rule the city, except that it was made up of mostly women who bickered constantly.

The witches were grouped by families, with four of the largest holding the most power among the faction. There was one group descended from the gypsies of Romania. Another group came from a long line of witches from France, one from Ireland, and another from the United Kingdom.

The smaller witch families were a mishmash of heritage, but that didn't make them any less dangerous.

Though Skye was curious about the witch faction, she was more focused on all the other beings that called New Orleans home. She also wanted to know what it was about the city that drew them.

Her next article was due in three days. Since she'd discovered so much about the Djinn by visiting the Viper's Nest, she thought it would be smart to return.

She pulled her phone from her purse and sent a text to Matthew to make sure he was free that night. He replied that he was.

"Fill up before I get there," she said aloud as she typed the words.

Matthew was a vampire, and she had no interest in being his meal. She still couldn't believe she had a vampire as a source. Even she rolled her eyes at the thought. What Skye wasn't sure about, was why Matthew wanted to help her. Exposing the supernatural also exposed him.

The one thing Skye did know was that she didn't trust him. Matthew had been helpful so far, especially by keeping others away from her at the bar. Still, he scared her.

However, a story was a story. And she had a whopper of one. If that meant she had to sit next to a vampire some nights while in the middle of a club full of other supernatural beings, she could do it.

Besides, she wore a silver necklace at all times. A thick silver chain.

She might be weaker than most, but she knew how to stop a vampire. It was something she'd learned while in college. A lesson that had sunk deep.

~ ~ ~

"What?" Solomon shouted.

Court winced at his eldest brother's tone. "I'm just thankful Kane still reads the damn newspaper."

Solomon ran a hand down his face and sighed. Myles hadn't said a word from his chair behind his desk. Court stood by the door as Solomon paced Myles's office.

"Does this woman have a death wish?" Solomon asked.

Myles threw down his pencil. "Apparently."

"It's times like these that make me want to sit back and let the idiots that get themselves into these messes get whatever is coming." Solomon's big hands fisted at his sides as his anger grew. "How fucking stupid do you have to be to go meddling in the affairs of the supernatural?"

Court couldn't agree more, but he also couldn't stand by and let an innocent get hurt. "It won't be long before one of the factions realize that Ms. Skye Parrish is a reporter for The Times – Picayune."

"A newspaper that thankfully has cut its distribution drastically," Solomon mumbled.

Myles leaned back in his office chair. "It's down to three times a week for printed, but it goes out every day online."

"That's good news, right?" Solomon looked from Myles to Court.

Court shook his head. "Afraid not. It looks like subscription service has increased fifteen percent since her first article three weeks ago."

"Goddamn it!"

Myles flattened his lips for a moment. "She has to be stopped."

"We can't just tell her to stop," Court argued. "She'll want to know why. I'm a hundred percent certain none of us want our names in anything she writes."

Solomon rubbed his fingers back and forth over his forehead. "A full moon is coming. If that...woman...isn't brought to heel, there's no telling what she'll find out."

"I'm on it," Court told his brothers. "I'll be tracking her with the help of Kane and Riley."

At the mention of their brother, Myles's and

Solomon's eyes snapped to him. Court blew out a breath and pushed away from the wall.

"Kane is doing some research on Skye Parrish for us. Riley will be the connection we need to the reporter. Hopefully, to get her to back down."

Myles sat forward, his face creased in lines of worry. "It may take all of us."

"We're just visiting bars, Myles. The Viper's Nest and Boudreaux's. Besides, you and Solomon can take care of Gator Bait for a few nights."

Solomon had a perturbed look on his face as he turned to Myles. "What do you think?"

"I think they have it well enough in hand," Myles said. "All they'll be doing is tracking Skye for a few nights. If there is a problem, we can get to them fast enough."

There was a long stretch of silence before Solomon nodded as he slid his gaze to Court. "I don't need to tell you what will happen if Riley is hurt."

"She's the sister we never had. I'd never let anything happen to her," Court vowed.

Myles threw a pencil at him and grinned. "Get to it then. But first, it's your turn to accept the delivery out back."

Right at that moment, the bell at the back of the bar rang. Court left Myles's office to make his way to the kitchen to accept their daily delivery.

He glanced at the clock. Just a few more hours before he met with Kane to go over what he'd learned about Skye Parrish.

~ ~ ~

"There isn't much," Kane said from his spot at the kitchen table as he pushed the laptop toward Court.

Court made a face. "As if, Kane. There has to be something."

"He's not lying," Riley said from the bathroom.

Court glanced at his cousin to see her hand moving as she brushed out her hair. He returned his attention to Kane. "What did you find out?"

"She wasn't raised anywhere in the US that I can find."

"You had to have found something more," Court stated.

Riley leaned back to peer around the bathroom doorway and grinned. "Oh, we did."

There was a ghost of a smile as Kane pointed to the laptop. "I traced Skye Parrish backwards. She came to New Orleans from LA where she did a brief stint at the Los Angeles Times. Before that, she got her degree in journalism from UCLA."

"Where is she from though?" Court asked.

Kane waited a few seconds before he said, "The Bahamas."

Court was so surprised at the news that he sat back in his chair without anything to say.

"I know, right?" Riley said as she walked out of the bathroom. "I had that exact reaction. Who grows up in the Bahamas?"

Court blinked as he looked at his cousin in her dark jeans and bright pink shirt. The top dipped low enough to show ample cleavage. He didn't think she should be wearing anything like that going to the places they were headed.

"Wipe that look off your face right now, Court LaRue," she told him sternly. "I'm a grown woman who has lived by myself for years."

Court looked to Kane for help, but Kane was busy typing on his laptop again. Court gave up with a shake of his head. "Is that all you found out about Skye?"

"It seems Ms. Parrish came from a family with big connections. Her mother came from money, and her father was the CEO of a plastics corporation. She was born in New York, but the family made their permanent home in Nassau," Kane answered.

Riley walked to the sink and rinsed out a cup to load in the dishwasher. "I'd like to know why she left the cushy life. If her parents had that kind of money, why not use it?"

"They're dead."

Kane's statement had Court frowning. "When and how?"

"Her first year at UCLA." Kane leaned forward, his brow furrowed as his gaze scanned the computer screen. "I can't get to the police report, but the newspaper article states there was a car accident. Mr. Parrish was driving and the car flipped, going into the ocean. Both of Skye's parents were killed."

Riley stood next to Kane. "How tragic."

"It also appears the Parrishs didn't have as much money as they let on. All of their properties, cars, jewels, and most of their belongings had to be sold to cover their debt after their death."

Court couldn't imagine having that kind of money and then losing it. It made him look at Skye Parrish differently.

"That's about it, at least from what I could dig up," Kane said.

Court didn't believe that for a minute. "There's more. There's always more."

"That's what I'm for," Riley said. "I'll suss it out of her quick enough."

Kane looked up from the computer screen. "No doubt you will, Riley, but don't trust her. She's looking for a story. Any story."

"Heard. Loud and clear."

Court stood. "Time's a wastin'. Let's get moving. The sooner we find Skye Parrish, the sooner we can figure out what she's looking for."

Kane closed the laptop and got to his feet. "I think we should let Riley take the lead. You and I will hang back and observe."

"Sure."

The three left Kane's apartment. As soon as they reached the streets, Riley went ahead of them. They were staying in the French Quarter. If Skye wanted to find something, that's the place she would look.

Riley was about fifty steps in front of them. As he kept his eye on her, Court wondered how long it would take for the remaining Chiasson brothers to realize that Beau had found his sister weeks ago and was keeping it from the rest of them.

If Court were in their shoes, he would be

furious. Then again, Beau was looking out for his sister. He knew she was safe. That was the only reason he hadn't told his brothers.

What Riley didn't know was that Solomon and Beau talked every week. As long as Beau was getting regular reports on his sister, he would keep his mouth shut about where she was.

All Court could hope for was that Riley never found out what Solomon was doing. If she did, she might leave and then no one would know where she was. Given that she was a Chiasson with a need to fight the supernatural in her blood, she could get herself into all kinds of trouble.

"What's got you all sour?" Kane asked.

Court jerked his chin to Riley. "Her."

"We are some kind of blessed not to have had a sister." Kane blew out a long breath. "I can't imagine growing up with one. Riley is blood, but I didn't have to watch her growing up while keeping her away from the monsters – and men."

Court cut him a look. "Do you think it'll be any better if Myles and Addison ever have a daughter?"

"Oh shit. You just had to make me think of that." Kane gave a firm shake of his head. "I'm never having kids. Ever. Or a wife. I don't need that kind of constant worry and strain."

Court was nodding in agreement. Life was hard enough as a LaRue. Adding a female into the mix only complicated things further.

Myles had gotten lucky with Addison. Solomon...he hadn't been so fortunate. He knew firsthand the sorrow of being a LaRue in love.

Chapter Three

Skye kept her clothes simple and plain. She wanted to blend in and observe, not draw attention. She wore a black long-sleeved shirt with a cowlneck and black jeans. Her hair was pulled back in a low ponytail. She wore no jewelry other than her thick silver necklace, and she didn't carry a purse. Her cell phone was in her pocket, along with a few twenties.

"Still nervous?" Matthew asked from beside her.

They stood across the street from The Viper's Nest, a known vampire hangout. She gave Matthew a dark look, but inside, she was a shaking bundle of nerves.

She was petrified, though she would never let Matthew know just how much vampires scared her.

"A brave face," he murmured. "You're going to need it in there."

Skye took a deep breath. Humans went into the Viper's Nest all the time. Most came out just as they had gone in, but there were others who never came out at all. Some went in knowing exactly what the Viper's Nest was and were ready to willingly give their blood to a vamp.

She gagged at the thought. Why did movies and TV shows make vampires out to be sexy, romantic figures? They were monsters that fed off blood. And killed.

Without a conscience.

After waiting for a car to pass, Skye crossed the street and strode to the door of the Viper's Nest. Matthew reached the door before her and held it open.

She walked inside and was deafened by the music. It was hard rock, the kind where the singers screamed rather than sang. Matthew guided her to the left as she looked to the dance floor where a number of people were gyrating sexually.

Matthew suddenly jerked her to the right. Skye whirled around, ready to tell him not to be so rough, when she realized he'd moved her out of the way of a group of males who surrounded a young woman with blond hair. She was completely naked and letting them touch her. Everywhere.

Skye was shaking by the time she and Matthew reached the bar. She thought it would be a safe place, but there was no safe place in this club.

"We can leave now," Matthew leaned down to

say in her ear.

She wanted nothing more than to get to the door as fast as she could, but she'd promised Helen an article on the vampires. What had she been thinking? Oh, Skye knew exactly what had led her to agree to such a thing. It was seeing her name and picture next to the words she had written.

It was a heady thing, having a dream come true. Though it might very well lead to her death.

Skye shook her head. "I have to stay."

"It's a mistake," Matthew mumbled and ordered her a draft beer.

She knew it was a risk. Her editor knew exactly where she was going though, and there was a file that would automatically be sent to Helen if Skye didn't key in the password by eight A.M.

Journalists who went into the middle of a combat zone knew they might die. Skye was in the middle of a war herself. Only hers had supernatural beings such as vampires, Djinn, and witches. So far, she had steered clear of the Voodoo faction, and as far as she knew, she had yet to see any werewolves.

But both were on her list to get to know.

Skye made sure not to put her beer down. She drank it slowly as she made mental notes of everything about the club and the people in it.

She had no idea how long she'd sat there before she realized that Matthew was gone and her beer was empty. Skye set the glass aside and looked for Matthew, but he was nowhere to be found. She was about to get up and leave when two large men boxed her in. An uneasy feeling overtook her as she looked up into their faces.

They were dangerous looking, rough. She knew without having to be told that they were vampires. And, unfortunately, they had taken an interest in her.

Skye belatedly realized that one of them had been drinking from the neck of a Creole woman earlier. However, there was no sign of that woman now. The vampire's hair was black and thick as it hung to his chin. His eyes were beady, and the gold hoop earring in his left ear was mesmerizing.

"Going somewhere?" he asked.

Skye pointed to her drink. "I've had my limit, and I'm supposed to meet a friend down the street."

She tried to get up again, but they pushed her down, none too gently. Skye's heart pounded in her chest, dread turning her blood to ice.

"You want to be with us," said the second man.

She swiveled her head to him and forgot who or where she was for a moment. He had a look about him that spoke of ancient times, snow-capped mountains, and wealth. His hair was deep mahogany and parted on the side. He smiled crookedly, stroking her cheek.

"You do want to be with us, don't you?"

~ ~ ~

"Damn," Court said when he saw Skye nod her head at the vampire.

Kane touched his arm and slipped out of the

bar. Court managed to reach Riley before she got close to Skye. He turned his cousin to the door and put her in a position that would allow her to leave in a hurry if needed.

Court remained in the bar. For the past two hours, he had been watching Skye Parrish study everyone. She was so intent on catching every detail that she'd missed the most crucial one – the fact that she was drawing attention to herself.

The man who'd stood beside her most of the night had left without a word. Court couldn't wait to get his hands on the bastard. Only the slimiest of assholes left a woman defenseless, especially in a place like the Viper's Nest.

Skye had drawn the attention of two of the most powerful vampires in the bar. Many of the vamps were trying to get near her, but the two with her now had stopped any of the others from getting close.

The wolf within Court yearned to be free, wanted to clamp his jaws down on their throats. The need was so overwhelming that Court found himself about to shift right there.

He shook his head and focused on Skye. The two vamps had her on her feet, flanking her as they walked her to the door. If they got her out of the bar, there was a chance they could spirit her away, and that would be the end of Skye Parrish.

Court waited for them to pass before he set aside his full glass of beer and followed them. He stopped the door before it closed on him and stepped out into the humid night air.

The vampires were so intrigued by their new catch they had no idea Court was following them, or that Kane was on one side of the street while Riley was on the other.

For the next four blocks, Court slowly gained on them until he was only a couple of steps behind. Suddenly, the tall vamp with the gold earring whirled around.

Jacques' eyes blazed for a moment before he recognized Court. "What do you want, wolf?"

"The woman."

The two vampires laughed. Court joined in while Skye stood silently staring straight ahead, completely unaware of what was going on around her.

"I'm not kidding," Court said.

Anton turned to the side and tilted his head. "The Viper's Nest is neutral territory."

"That doesn't mean you can forcefully leave with a human."

"She wants to come with us," Jacques argued.

Court lifted a brow as he looked at Skye. "Right. And you didn't use your mind control to get her to do what you wanted."

Anton wrapped his arm around Skye and turned her so that she faced Court. "We're not making her do anything. Ask her."

Skye's eyes weren't dilated or unfocused. She met Court's gaze. "I want to go with them."

"What's your name?" he asked her.

Jacques stepped in front of Skye. "Why can't you believe that some humans want to be with us?"

"Because some of them might not want to have all of their blood drained or to become a vampire," Court retorted.

Anton pulled Skye closer to him. "By the rules of the city, if she wants to come with us, you can't interfere."

The two vampires began to turn around, taking Skye with them again. Court didn't know how they had gotten Skye to comply so easily, but he wasn't going to stand by and let the vamps take her.

"Release her. Now," Court demanded.

Jacques turned, his lips peeled back to show his fangs as he hissed. Kane ran from across the street and rammed a shoulder into Jacques, sending both of them crashing into a store window. Glass shattered everywhere.

Anton dropped his arm from around Skye and glared at Court. "You've made a deadly mistake, wolf. Now you'll pay for it with your life."

Court dodged the vampire's fangs and jammed his fist in Anton's stomach. He tried to keep the vampire away from Skye, but Anton kept trying to reach her and throw her over his shoulder.

With no other choice, Court fought near the woman who stood staring blankly at them. Court got off two quick punches to Anton's face as they circled each other. He was ready to land a third when Anton stepped back, right into Skye.

They toppled over with Anton landing heavily upon Skye. As much as Court wanted to kill the vampire, he couldn't. Not without proof that they'd used some kind of magic on Skye.

While he couldn't kill the bloodsucker, he could beat him plenty. He jerked Anton off Skye. With every punch he landed, Court felt better. There was nothing like beating up on a vampire.

Suddenly, both Anton and Jacques were gone. Court wiped the blood from his split lip as he looked at Kane, who was bent over, his hands upon his knees.

Riley walked out of the shadows. "Three vampires paused long enough to see what was going on, but it was one of Delphine's people who was observing from the far corner that worries me."

"Let them watch," Kane said and straightened.

Court walked to Skye and knelt beside her. Her eyes were closed. She lay unmoving. He had the urge to take down her carefully styled black hair. Even more annoying, he had the irresistible urge to hear her voice.

"Is she all right?" Riley asked, concern deepening her voice.

Court gently turned Skye's head from one side to the other to look for blood. Thankfully, there was none. He tapped her cheek to wake her, but she didn't stir.

"What did they do to her?" Kane asked.

Riley made a sound at the back of her throat. "Whatever it is, it isn't good. We can't leave her out here."

"And we can't take her back to any of our places," Court pointed out.

Riley suddenly smiled. "I know where we can

take her. Follow me."

Court gathered Skye's petite frame in his arms and stood. He and Kane followed Riley to her car. After they were inside, Kane and Court began to try and figure out what the vamps had used to subdue Skye while Riley drove.

"It was something new," Court said.

Kane nodded grimly. "That's my worry. How many other women are they carting off that we don't know about?"

"Let's not think about that right now," Riley said. "We have Skye. She can tell us what happened and how it made her feel when she wakes up. That should help us figure out what it is. If we don't know, Minka will."

Court looked down at the woman in his arms. Skye had yet to move. She was breathing evenly, her golden skin warm beneath his hands.

"Is going to the witch wise?" Kane asked.

Riley gave him a dour look. "Have a better idea?"

Of course, Kane didn't. Neither did Court. He tried to look up from Skye's face, but his eyes kept getting drawn back down to her. She appeared asleep, innocent. The fact that she had no idea the shit storm she had created didn't turn him off. In fact, it's what interested him.

Her oval face was flawless. She was a classic beauty with her high cheekbones, gently arching black brows, and thick lashes. Her mouth, however, was a seduction all its own. Deep pink lips that were plump and wide.

Tempting lips, enticing lips.

Court ran the back of his fingers down her cheek. Skye might be delving into a world she should stay out of, but Court couldn't be angry that it had brought her into his life. She intrigued him.

Even if he knew nothing good could come of it.

CHAPTER FOUR

"...depends on how much."

"It depends on who created it."

Skye heard the voices, but she didn't recognize them. Her head pounded with every beat of her heart, making her a little nauseous. She tried to remain still and take stock of things. Especially since she didn't remember leaving the Viper's Nest.

"She's waking," said a male voice.

"About time," came a throaty female reply.

Skye didn't know how people could wake up and remain perfectly still. She had to move. Perhaps it was a learned trait that spies and military people were taught. Though, at this moment, she would have preferred to remain still and learn more about where she was and who was with her.

She opened her eyes and immediately turned

her head away from the lamplight that blinded her. Covering her eyes with her hand, she blinked and let things come into focus.

"There you are," came a friendly female voice.

Skye looked up to see a woman with long dark hair and bright blue eyes leaning over the back of the couch and smiling down at her.

"You took quite a fall," she continued.

Skye licked her dry lips. She couldn't remember falling. Hell, she couldn't remember much of anything other than sitting in the bar and realizing that Matthew was gone. The bastard.

He'd left her!

Fury spiked through her. She sat up, immediately grabbing her head as the pounding intensified. Her stomach rolled violently.

The couch dipped next to her as the same female said, "Here, this will help."

Skye looked down to see two aspirin in the palm of the woman's hand. Since she couldn't think straight with her head hurting so bad, Skye accepted the pills and tossed them in her mouth.

Next, a tall glass of iced tea was put in front of her. Skye took it and drank deeply, loving the taste of the sweet tea as she swallowed the pills.

"Where am I?" she asked. With her elbow braced on her thigh, she carefully lowered her head into her hand. Her voice sounded hoarse, weak. How she hated that.

"Safe," replied the woman. "I'm Riley, by the way."

Skye turned her head to look at Riley. "What

happened?"

Riley hesitated, her gaze dropping to the floor for a moment. "What's the last thing you remember?"

"Being at the bar."

"The Viper's Nest isn't a nice place. You shouldn't have been there."

Skye lifted her head to find the source of the male voice, and found the man sitting at a table in the kitchen looking severe and angry. There was a woman with dark curly hair and brown eyes sitting next to him.

These people were strangers. She was in a strange place, with no memory of how she had gotten there. She needed to get out. Now.

"We're friends," Riley said and put her hand atop Skye's. "We rescued you from the men trying to make you leave with them and brought you here."

Skye frowned. There's no way she would have left with men she didn't know. That wasn't like her. Especially from a bar like the Viper's Nest with all those vampires.

Her stomach plummeted to her feet. Vampires. Oh, God. Matthew had left her with all those vampires. Why would he do that? He was getting paid plenty to escort her around such places and ensure she was protected.

"She's remembering," said the man at the table.

Skye ignored him as she closed her eyes. She searched her mind, trying to fill in the time she was missing between realizing Matthew was gone and waking up here.

"It's as if there's a window blocking those memories," she explained. "Like it's iced over so thick I can't see through it. I know there are people on the other side, but I can't make them out."

"What about voices?"

This came from a second male. She recognized the voice. She had heard it when she was waking. A shiver raced through her at the rich, seductive sound of it. It took her a moment to focus back on her thoughts. "I can hear someone talking, but I can't tell what is being said."

Skye opened her eyes and turned to where the man's voice had come from. He was sitting half in the shadows where the light from the lamp didn't quite reach. Though she couldn't make out his face, she could tell he was staring at her.

She swallowed, entranced by the stranger. He drew not just her gaze but her total concentration. So much so that she forgot they weren't alone in the room.

He sat still as stone, his hands resting on the arms of the chair. He gave off the impression that he was at ease, but she had the sense that he could be up and ready to face whatever came through the door in an instant.

Their gazes locked and held for several quiet moments. Skye couldn't look away, no matter how many times she tried. There was something so...beguiling about him. The thread of danger, of something dark and primal, couldn't be ignored.

She jerked when she saw his eyes flash yellow.

Skye blinked and rubbed her eyes. She was mistaken. She had to be. A man's eyes, hidden in shadow, couldn't flash yellow. It was absurd.

You hit your head, remember?

Yes. Her head. She had hit her head. That's why she was seeing things that weren't there. The explanation was enough to calm her racing heart.

"I'd like to leave," she told the room at large and lifted her head.

Riley looked at the man in the shadowed corner before she turned her head to the table.

"Not going to happen," said the man at the table.

The woman next to him glared at him, one brow raised. "She's not staying here, Kane."

Riley got to her feet when Kane opened his mouth to argue. "Skye, the one glaring is my cousin, Kane. This is Minka," she said pointing to the woman. "And you're in her house." There was a short pause before Riley looked to the other man. "The silent one in the corner is Kane's brother, Court."

Skye hated how badly she wanted to see Court's face. She told herself it was because she wanted a good look at the people who'd helped her, but she knew it was more primal than that.

Then she frowned at Riley as she stood, her knees beginning to shake. "You know my name." How was that possible? Skye didn't have any identification on her. Nothing that would tell someone who she was.

"I think we should ease her into it," Riley told

Kane.

Kane made a face like Riley had asked him to pluck a cloud from the sky. "Ease her into it? She already jumped."

"She would like to know what the hell is going on," Skye said, looking at each of them in turn. "How do you know my name?"

Court leaned forward in the chair so that his forearms rested on his knees. She caught a glimpse of chin-length butterscotch blond hair. "Of course, we know who you are. By what happened tonight, others know you're the one writing the articles about them, as well."

It was everything Skye could do to remain standing. "You think someone attacked me tonight?"

"That's one way of putting it," Kane mumbled.

Riley rolled her eyes and faced Skye. "We think the articles might have upset some."

Skye took a step back from Riley. "Why do you care about the articles?"

"Look at what happened tonight. You should be worried," Minka said as she rose gracefully from the chair. She wore jeans and a willowy white shirt that brought out her mocha skin. She walked past Skye to a door that led out onto a porch. "You stepped into something you had no business digging around in. Now you've put a target on yourself."

The only kinds of people that would be upset about what she wrote were the ones who actually believed. Or the ones who were part of the supernatural.

Skye turned her head to watch Minka and saw the glint of moonlight off water filtered through trees. The bayou. They had brought her out of the city.

"We're not going to hurt you," Riley said in a soft voice, as if reading Skye's thoughts. "We had to get you out of the city in case they came back for you."

Skye rubbed her temple, hoping that would help stop some of the pain. "Tell me what happened. Please."

"You went into the Viper's Nest," Kane said, his voice dripping with derision. "You knew it would be filled with vampires, and yet you willingly went in there alone."

She took exception to that. "I'm not stupid. I wasn't alone. I had someone with me."

"He left you," Court said.

Skye handed Riley the rest of her sweet tea and started out the door Minka had exited. It didn't matter how far she was from the city. She wasn't staying there any longer.

She reached the porch and was turning to tell them just that when Court stood in front of her. The moon hit him square in the face, showing her the hard line of his jaw, the firm contours of his cheekbones, and blue eyes so vivid they were almost electric. He was so tall she had to tilt her head back to look at him. There was space between them, but there was no denying the pure power she saw displayed by the tee that clung to his wide shoulders and thick arms and chest.

He held up his hands, palms out. "Easy, Skye. We brought you here because the vampires were intent on leaving with you. We stopped them, but I know Jacques and Anton well enough to know that they'll come looking for you again. They've singled you out."

Out of the corner of her eye, she saw Riley and Kane standing in the doorway to her right. To her left and behind her, Minka stood at the railing of the porch looking out over the bayou.

Court sighed and dropped his hands. "We need to know how the vamps got you to leave with them. Tell us that and I'll drive you back to the city myself."

"I don't remember anything," she said, frustration growing with every second. She cocked her head to the side. "Why do you have interest in the vampires? Most people don't believe they're real."

At that moment, a howl sounded. A howl that was very wolf-like. Skye glanced around her. There were no wolves in the parish, which meant it was a werewolf. She looked at Court with new eyes. Were he and Kane werewolves?

"You live in New Orleans long enough, you see everything," Court answered.

It was the biggest line of shit Skye had heard all week. She didn't call him out on it though. Not yet. She wanted to know more about him.

Kane crossed his arms over his chest. "You don't remember anything, my ass. Lady, you've got some nerve. We save your scrawny hide, and you want to give us the runaround."

"I'm not," she said defensively as she looked at him. "I'm trying to figure things out. You're the ones who took me out of the city. Maybe it's you I should be afraid of."

"You're right. It was us that took you," Court said, a hard edge to his voice. "But we didn't lead you out of the club. That was the vampires."

Skye shook her head. "I wouldn't have left with them. I drank my beer and I was getting up to leave. Then I woke up here."

"Someone could've spiked her beer," Riley suggested.

Skye was shaking her head before she finished. "I never set my drink down. I know better."

"The witches wouldn't be involved," Minka said. "So don't even think of blaming them, Kane."

Kane shot her a dark look. "I put blame where blame goes."

With a loud sigh, Minka turned to them. "The witches aligned with the werewolves to take down..." She paused and glanced at Skye. "To do that thing. That was the exception to the rule. The witches never align with anyone."

"She's right," Court said. "The witches wouldn't help the vampires."

Minka lifted her chin, a small smile about her lips. "Then there is that."

Skye felt as if she were in a dream where everyone talked around her, excluding her on purpose.

"That leaves the Djinn and weres," Kane said.

Riley chuckled. "We can cross out the weres."

"Magic was used," Minka said. "That's the only explanation."

Skye's mind was in a whirl. "Wait. I thought vampires could use some kind of mind control on their victims."

"They can," Court said. "But it isn't allowed."

She couldn't help but laugh. "Allowed? These are vampires we're talking about."

"Who are strictly controlled within the city," Riley said.

Kane looked away from her with distaste. "Something you forgot to mention in your articles."

"I didn't mention it because I didn't know. I'm still learning."

Court said, "Which is what almost got you killed tonight."

"I had Matthew," she said. "I pay him to accompany me to places like the Viper's Nest and keep others away."

Minka tucked a long, dark curl behind her ear. "Why would you take Matthew? Who is he?"

"I took him because he's..." Even though there had been talk of all the factions, Skye was embarrassed to state what Matthew was.

Kane yawned. "Spit it out."

"He's a vampire," Skye said and made a face at Kane.

She was reduced to acting childish with a grown man who despised her. When was the nightmare going to end?

Court's phone vibrated. He pulled it out of his pocket and read the text.

Skye shifted her feet. "Look. I've answered your questions, and I'm obviously no help. I need to get back to the city and look for Matthew. He's never left me before, and I'm going to demand my money back."

"Don't bother," Court said as he lowered his phone and looked at her with his gorgeous eyes. "Matthew is dead. The police found him three blocks from the club with all his blood drained."

Skye blinked, not understanding. "Since when do vampires drink the blood of another vampire?"

"They don't," Minka said.

Kane dropped his arms, his nostrils flaring as he blew out a breath. "Matthew was human."

CHAPTER FIVE

It was clear to Court that Skye was shocked at the news that Matthew wasn't a vampire. He took a half-step toward her when her eyes went wide.

"That's not possible," she mumbled.

That got Minka's attention. "Why not?"

As if Skye realized she had spoken out loud, she shook her head. "I need to get back to the city."

"Hold on," Riley said. "What made you think Matthew was a vampire?"

Court watched Skye closely. He was mesmerized by the curve of her jaw and her amazing mouth. Her smooth skin glowed in the moonlight, making him want to stroke her face again.

Her throat moved as she swallowed, and she glanced at the bayou again. "I've done research."

But Court knew it was more than that. By the way Skye refused to look at anyone, he suspected she'd had a run-in with a vamp before.

"What research?" Kane asked with a sneer. "Movies? Watching them in their club?"

Court shot his brother a dark look. He understood why Kane had become a hard, easily angered person, but Skye didn't. Court caught Skye's gaze. "I'll drive you home."

"I know you all think I'm crazy, but I have to write these articles," Skye said. "People need to know what's out there."

Minka turned her back to the porch railing and crossed her arms over her chest. "You really think that? How do you think the city would be if everyone knew about vampires and witches? Do you think we would still be a mecca for tourism? Do you think everyone would just continue on as they are?"

"There would be chaos," Kane added.

Riley nodded. "Riots, too. Not to mention murders. Everyone would fear their neighbor, worry they might be a monster."

Skye's spine was straight as she listened to them. She didn't cower, didn't agree. Which made Court think that something had happened to her. If he could find out what that was, it would help him understand her and her need to report on the supernatural.

Kane said, "You need to stop the articles."

When Skye didn't bother to respond, Court held out his hand to Riley for the keys. She sent a troubled looked to Skye as she handed them over.

Court gave a nod of thanks to Minka and turned to walk around the porch and down the stairs. He would be back to pick up Riley and Kane, unless Kane took to the woods with the Moonstone wolves.

Once Skye was buckled in the seat of the truck, she crossed her arms over her chest and stared out the windshield. Court started the engine and backed up the vehicle before driving through the grass between the trees.

"How are you feeling?" he asked.

"The aspirin has dulled most of the pain."

He recalled how hard she had hit the pavement. "You're likely to have quite the bump."

"I already do."

Court inhaled deeply and swerved to miss a skunk and her three babies, causing him to drive around a group of live oaks.

"Thank you," Skye said. "I didn't say that back there. I know that makes me look ungrateful."

"You were on the defensive. I understand."

Her head turned to him. "Do you? Why? Why did you help me? Why were you even at the Viper's Nest?"

With as smart of a journalist as Skye was, Court knew he had to answer her or take his chances that she'd find out on her own. Perhaps if he made his case well enough, she might back off. It was a long shot, but one he had to take.

"I was there because of you." He glanced at her, the truck rocking as they drove through a muddy section. There was just enough ambient light for him to see her brow rise.

"For me?" she repeated, shaking her head. She returned her gaze forward. "Let me guess. The articles?" she asked, her voice dripping with sarcasm.

Court grinned despite the situation. Skye's annoyed tone sounded so similar to Riley's. "We're not the only ones who are noticing you. As you know, New Orleans is a dangerous city."

"Why are you interested in my articles? The truth, if you please."

"We told you back at the house. You're bringing attention to yourself that is going to get you killed."

"I've thought of that. There are contingencies in place for the police to track down my killer – no matter what or who it is."

Court pulled the truck onto the dirt road. "Seriously? That's your answer? You're a piece of work. We're trying to help you."

"No. You're stifling the people's right to know."

Court slammed on the brakes, and Skye's head snapped toward him. He jerked his head to her, tired of playing it nice. It was time she had the hard truth. "If you paid a little more attention to things, you might realize the supernatural extends far past a few sections of the city. They're inside political offices and every law enforcement agency of the city. So no, Skye, no one would look for your killer. You'd be another statistic in a long line of unsolved murders."

She blinked at him.

Court faced forward, his hands gripping the steering wheel. "You're up to your ass in a bad situation. Had we not been there tonight, the vamps would've taken you. Whether they wanted to feed off you or turn you, I don't know. Either way, you would no longer be the person you are now."

"It happened in college," she said softly.

Court swiveled his head toward Skye to find her looking down at her hands. He was silent, waiting for her to continue.

"I knew my roommate, Jo, was a bit different. I just thought she was goth. I didn't find out until we had lived in the dorms for almost a year that she was a witch."

Skye laughed, the sound forced as she rubbed her hands up and down her arms. "Jo didn't hide it exactly, but she didn't announce it either. I kept to myself most times, so I didn't pay attention to her much. We ran in different social circles too, but she was nice, and we got along."

"Until," Court urged when she stopped talking.

Skye looked at him. "It was during Christmas break. I had nowhere to go, and she chose to take an extra course during that time. It was late. She was up studying, and I had just gotten back from a date. That's when it walked into our dorm room."

"A vampire," Court guessed.

Skye nodded and glanced down. "I was so terrified I couldn't move. Since I was closer, he came at me first. Jo knew what he was, even if I didn't. She used a spell, along with silver to keep him from me. But he was determined to have one of us."

Court reached over and placed his hand on hers, giving Skye what little comfort he could. It may have happened years ago, but it obviously still affected her.

"Jo was so brave," Skye said with a smile. "I could only sit there and watch as she battled him. I never thought he would leave, but eventually she won. For the next two weeks, she told me everything she knew about the supernatural. I made notes, bought as much silver jewelry as I could, and soaked up everything she told me."

Skye paused and shifted in her seat. "One night, I came back to our room with an armload of books on the occult from the library only to find the room empty except for her silver necklace lying broken in the middle of the room. The police found her body three days later completely drained of blood."

"The vamp got her," Court said. "As powerful a witch as Jo was, she was overtaken by a vampire. That should tell you something."

Skye wiped at her eyes and sniffed. "I've been focused on the supernatural ever since. I had no idea vampires were real until that day. So many books and movies romanticize them, when in fact, they're monsters."

"They're beings who were once human. They were turned, whether willingly or by force," he told her. "Not all vampires are monsters. They do need blood to survive, but there are those in New Orleans who don't kill. Those vamps get their food supply from humans who willingly give their blood to the vampires. In return, the vamps pay them well and give them protection."

Skye made a sound. "Who would they need protection from? The worst monster is now their friend."

"There's the Djinn, witches, werewolves, and more importantly, there is Delphine."

"I've heard that name," Skye said with a small frown. "She's a Voodoo priestess, right?"

Court nodded as he pressed the accelerator and began driving again. "Stay far away from her, Skye. Trust me when I say you don't want to be on her radar. She's lethal and has no compunction about killing you on a crowded street."

"Noted."

"So you came to New Orleans to expose the supernatural." He shook his head, still unable to believe it. "That takes some balls."

She smiled and faced forward. "I told you my story. You still haven't told me why you're so concerned about what I put in my articles."

"Off the record?" he asked, glancing at her. She would find out all about his family with a little digging anyway.

"Off the record," Skye confirmed.

He rested one hand atop the steering wheel and put the other on the gearshift. "We keep the peace in the city."

"We?"

"Me and my three brothers."

She smoothed a hand over her slicked backed ponytail. "You're a supernatural being, aren't you?"

"Yep." He spared her another quick look to gauge her reaction. She didn't seem the least bit surprised. "Figure out what kind yet?"

Riley shrugged. "A matter of deduction, really. You're not a vampire or a Djinn. You don't look the type to practice Voodoo, nor are you a witch. That leaves...werewolf."

He was impressed. "Are you scared?"

"Should I be?"

Court laughed. "With that attitude, you just might make it out of New Orleans alive."

"Who said anything about leaving?"

He drove onto the highway. "You really want to risk your life to report on the craziness of the city?"

"I'd be dead if it hadn't been for Jo," she argued.

"You'd be dead tonight if it hadn't been for me." Court flattened his lips. "No matter how much you know about the supernatural, you're still not prepared to defend yourself."

. CHAPTER SIX

As dawn came and the sky turned a brilliant pink and gold, all Skye could think about was what Court had said to her. As much as she hated to admit it, he was right.

She'd assumed because Jo had taught her a few things that she was more than capable of doing research on the supernatural. What the previous night had taught her was that she only knew a thimbleful of what was out there.

Coffee in hand, Skye stood at the windows of her townhouse and looked out over the streets of the city. Vampires had almost kidnapped her. If not for Court and the others, Skye wouldn't be standing there now.

It galled her that she hadn't been able to take care of herself. She hadn't looked the vamps in the eye for more than a second, so she knew they hadn't used mind control on her. No one had spiked her drink. The vampires had touched her, that was the only thing that happened.

Skye jerked so hard the coffee spilled over the rim of the mug and burned her hand. She hissed and rushed barefoot into the kitchen to set the coffee down and wipe her hand.

Then she ran to her desk and tapped the keyboard to wake up her laptop. She might not know Court's last name, but she had enough skill to find him.

Thirty minutes later, she sat back with a smile on her face. "Court LaRue. Looks like I'm going to be paying you a visit at Gator Bait."

Skye got up from her chair and was headed into the bathroom to take a shower when her cell phone rang. She glanced at the phone to see it was her editor, Helen.

"Sorry, Helen. I can't talk right now," she said as she declined the call.

Turning on her music through her phone, Skye started the shower. She was taking off her sleep shirt when her phone dinged with a text. Skye tossed her sleep shirt on the bed and hurried into the bathroom where her phone rested on the counter.

She read the message, frowning as she did. Helen never demanded she come into the office when she was writing a story. What was going on?

Skye quickly texted back that she was in the middle of research and would try to get there later that day.

"Before lunch," Skye read Helen's reply aloud.

What the hell was going on?

Skye showered and got ready. Forty minutes later, she was walking out the door and headed to the newspaper. A short fifteen-minute stroll and she was at the office.

No sooner had Skye entered Helen's office than her editor rose and closed the door behind her. "What's going on?" Skye asked as she took one of the two chairs.

Helen sat down behind her desk and shoved her reading glasses on her head. She let out a long sigh. "Where were you last night?"

"Observing the supernatural." Skye didn't feel the need to lie to Helen. Yet, anyway.

Her editor leaned back in her chair and smoothed down her navy and white striped blouse. "Were you alone?"

Shit, shit, shit. In all the turmoil, Skye had completely forgotten about Matthew. She kept her expression blank. "Matthew went with me to a club, but he left me there."

"When did you arrive at the club?"

"About ten-ish."

Helen nodded. "And when did Matthew leave you?"

Skye shrugged, not liking the questions. "It was about midnight, I think. He always stays in the background. He could've left much earlier than I noticed. Why?" she added since she didn't want to admit what a failure she was in spotting supernatural beings.

"What did you do when you discovered that Matthew was gone?"

Skye scooted to the end of the chair. "Why does this feel like an interrogation?"

"Please answer me, Skye."

"I stayed until it became uncomfortable and then I left."

"Alone?"

There was something about the way Helen said it that made Skye aware her boss knew something. Once again, she decided on the truth. Mostly. "I tried to leave on my own, but two vampires attempted to get me to go with them. Two guys and a girl helped me out. They walked me home, and here I am."

"Good. Those are good answers. You'll do fine, Skye," Helen said as she leaned forward and rested her arms on the desk.

"Do fine?" Skye repeated. "What's that mean?"

Helen's face pinched in worry. "I hate to be the one to tell you this, but Matthew was found dead this morning."

Even though Skye knew he was dead, hearing it again was like a punch to the gut. She looked down, feeling sick. "How?" she croaked out.

"The police are calling it a homicide. They think it was an attempted robbery, and assume Matthew tried to resist. His attacker used a knife."

Skye could only stare at Helen. The police were covering it up. Aside from saving her, Court had given her no reason to trust him, but what he'd said about the supernatural in law enforcement made sense.

"They're going to want to talk to you," Helen was saying.

Skye mentally shook herself. "How do they even know my connection to Matthew?"

"Someone at the club said they saw the two of you enter together."

Just freaking wonderful. Skye wished she had remained in the bayou with Court instead of insisting that she return to the city.

"I see."

"I wanted to let you know so you wouldn't be surprised."

Skye ran her hands through her hair. "Should I go to the police?"

"There's no need yet," Helen said. "They'll find you if they want to talk to you."

Skye stood then. "I need to finish some research for the article."

"Stay in touch," Helen said.

Skye walked out of the office on shaky legs. Not even the fresh air calmed her. She spotted a patrol car driving slowly down the street, and she remained where she was, waiting for them to come for her.

It drove past.

She released a relieved breath and turned to the left. It was time to visit Court. Even in late September, the streets were crowded with tourists. October was a truly crazy month for New Orleans since everyone equated the city at Halloween with the supernatural.

It was all the innocents walking around that had prompted her to write the articles. The college kids just looking to get lucky, the high schoolers looking to score some alcohol, the families just wanting to make lasting memories, and the business professionals wanting to have some fun.

Those were the people the supernatural hunted.

Or so she'd thought before last night. Court had said some of the vampires didn't kill. The thought boggled her mind. A vampire that didn't kill? How was that even possible? And who made the laws?

Court mentioned that his family enforced the laws, but how could four brothers control an entire city of supernatural when a thousand policemen couldn't govern the humans?

Skye spotted the LaRue's bar situated at the corner of the street. The wooden sign hung above the sidewalk with a bite taken out of the side, as if by an alligator. The lettering was done in a deep green with a gator below the name, its mouth wide open.

It was after noon, and already, the bar was busy. The sound of music thumping could be heard even from outside. It wasn't until customers walked from the bar that she recognized Godsmack playing.

Skye glanced at her reflection in the window before she stepped inside Gator Bait. As soon as she entered, she stopped and looked around.

The place was welcoming with its wood floors

and highly polished bar. Hundreds of pictures of celebrities who had visited lined the walls. There were also alligator jaws of various sizes hung here and there.

All in all, it looked like Court.

"Court said you would come?" Riley said as she walked up with a smile.

Skye returned her grin, intrigued that Court would know her well enough to announce what she would do. "Did he?"

"He's insufferably right most of the time," Riley said with a wink.

Skye laughed at the remark. Whatever she might think of the LaRues, they were obviously a close-knit family.

"You hungry?" Riley asked as she motioned Skye to follow her. "We've got the best gator in town."

"Sure." Skye's stomach rumbled, reminding her the banana she'd had for breakfast was long gone.

Skye took a seat at the bar and watched two men playing pool. Riley wasn't the only waitress at the bar. There were three others, and all were busy.

A man with ash blond hair walked out from the kitchen with papers in hand and a pencil in his mouth. His blue eyes, as well as the shape of his face, reminded Skye so much of Court that she knew this had to be another LaRue brother.

He walked to a woman with jaw-length champagne blond hair and took the pencil out of his mouth to whisper something in her ear. She laughed and gave him a quick kiss.

"That's Addison."

Skye jumped at the sound of Riley's voice. She turned and found a glass of beer in front of her.

"Addison and Myles are engaged," Riley continued.

Skye tasted the beer and nodded in approval. "Does she know everything?"

"Yep." Riley grinned. "It's a long story. Suffice it to say, Addison had a crash course in it."

"Ah. I'm surprised it's not kept more secret."

Riley tucked her hair behind her ear. "If people want to know the truth, they're going to go looking for it whether we want them to or not."

"Are you...?" Skye asked, not quite able to spit it out.

Riley chuckled and pulled at her black shirt with the Gator Bait logo. "Nope. That's contained to the LaRues. I'm just a normal girl who keeps the supernatural in line. My brothers live a couple hours away."

"But they know?"

"Of course." Riley walked around the bar and came to sit beside Skye. "I'm going to just put it out there because you obviously want to know. The Chiassons, my immediate family, came to Louisiana from France with a stop in Nova Scotia. They were hunters of the supernatural. The ones that kill innocents anyway."

Skye was listening raptly.

"There were two brothers and one sister. The sister came to New Orleans and married a LaRue. One brother chose to go west, and the other settled in Lyons Point, outside of Lafayette, which is a hotbed of supernatural activity. All of us, both the Chiassons and LaRues, are raised to protect the innocent and kill the monsters."

"But the LaRues are werewolves."

Riley lifted one shoulder in a shrug. "That they are. If you want that story, you'll have to ask Court. The point is, the LaRues have always kept the peace in New Orleans. Before they were cursed and after. That's never changed."

"Nor will it," said a voice behind Skye.

She turned and found Court. If she'd thought him handsome by the light of the moon, he took her breath away in the daytime. He was startlingly good-looking. The kind of gorgeous that left a woman speechless.

His chin-length hair was parted down the middle, the butterscotch blond strands having a slight wave as they framed his face. His brilliant blue eyes were just as powerful as before.

Skye glanced down and saw that he was wearing a pair of jeans, slung low on his narrow hips, and a cream henley shirt with a big bronze fleur de lis on the upper right side by his shoulder.

"I told you she'd come, Riley," Court said without taking his gaze from Skye.

Riley slid off the barstool and paused beside Skye long enough to say, "He's conceited. Feel free to bring him down a notch or two."

Skye couldn't help but smile. Court was self-assured. It showed in the way he held himself and how he greeted the world. Conceited? Skye didn't know him well enough to say, but she could see it was a possibility.

"Why did you think I'd come?"

Court took her beer in one hand and grabbed her hand with the other, pulling her off the stool. He led her through the doorway into the back, but it wasn't the kitchens he brought her to. It was an office.

"You're curious," he said. "I knew you would want to know more."

He wasn't wrong. Apparently, she was easy to figure out. Skye frowned. That wasn't a good thing, was it?

Her thoughts stopped when she was shown a chair and given her beer. Court took the seat next to her the same time Myles walked in reading over some papers with the pencil once more in his mouth.

He didn't look up at them even as he sat behind the desk and keyed something in the computer. A few minutes later, Kane and another man entered the office.

So, these were the four LaRue brothers.

Court hadn't lied. She was up to her neck in werewolves now.

CHAPTER SEVEN

Court watched Skye carefully. Her entire body tightened when Kane and Solomon entered the room. Solomon ran a hand through his dark blond hair as he leaned against the corner of Myles's desk.

"I'm sure you've done some checking on us, but I'm Solomon," he said. He motioned with his thumb over his shoulder. "The one buried in the computer doing the accounting for this place is Myles. You've already met Kane and Court."

Skye held Solomon's gaze. "I have done my checking. I know that you're the eldest, followed by Myles, Kane, and then Court. You four have owned Gator Bait for years now and are upstanding citizens in all ways. And you have a very big secret."

"Everyone has secrets," Kane said, eyeing her.

"Everyone."

Skye crossed one leg over the other. "I do have a secret. I shared it with Court last night."

"He told us," Myles said as he set aside his pencil. "That's one hell of a story."

Court's balls tightened when Skye glanced at him. Damn but she was a beautiful woman. It wasn't just her beauty that drew him, it was her courage and nerve – even if she had been foolish to go into the Viper's Nest.

"It is." Skye licked her lips and let her gaze land on each one of them. "I told Court last night, but I want to say it here. Thank you for helping me. I thought I knew enough to handle myself. I was wrong."

Court didn't know who was more surprised by her words, him or Kane. He merely smiled at Skye because the woman was good. The fact that she could admit she was wrong, right after thanking them meant there was no way any of them was going to get on her case now.

"My editor called me into the office this morning," Skye said. "She says the police are calling Matthew's death a homicide and saying that he was killed with a knife."

Solomon rubbed his chin as he considered Skye. "I saw Matthew's body myself. There was no denying the holes in his neck, or the fact that all his blood was gone."

"We're not the ones lying here," Court said.

Skye's dark brown gaze turned to him. "I know. It's just a lot to take in. I assumed every human was innocent."

Kane snorted but didn't make a comment.

Court could only imagine how she felt with her world turned upside down. "The witches are human, and not all of them are innocent."

"Minka is," Myles said.

Court nodded in agreement, even as he saw Solomon's jaw tighten at the mention of the witch. Court really hoped his eldest brother could get over whatever was eating at him when it came to Minka. Having a witch as an ally was something Court didn't want ruined.

"This is my job," Skye said. "I'm paid to write these articles, and the only way to do that is by gaining information."

Myles made a face. "Not if it means your death."

"We're trying to keep you alive," Court said. "You have to choose what to do. If you go back to the Viper's Nest, we may not be there next time."

She squared her shoulders. "I understand. I also came here because I think I remember something about what happened last night."

Court sat forward. "What?"

"I told you I guard my drink well. I also know never to look a vampire in the eye in case they use their mind control." She paused for a moment. "What I do remember is one of the vampires touching me. After that, my memory is blank until I woke up at Minka's."

Court got to his feet and paced. "They touched her. No way a vamp can use their mind control that way."

"They have to make eye contact," Myles added.

Solomon's hands tightened on the desk. "Someone has to be helping the vampires."

"Just what we need," Kane mumbled.

Court stopped beside Skye's chair and squatted. "What did the vampires say to you exactly?"

"I don't remember," she said with a shrug. "I've been thinking about it all night."

Solomon straightened. "It doesn't matter. We have what we need. We must find who is helping the vampires. It's never a good thing when two factions align."

"You knew it would come to this," Kane said.

Court stood and put a hand on Kane's shoulder. "We had to get the witches to help us."

"Addison's life was at stake," Myles said sharply. "I would've welcomed anyone's help. We're lucky the witches agreed to join forces with us."

By the way Skye looked between them, Court knew she was going to ask about it later.

"What can I do to help?" Skye asked.

Court was as taken aback by her offer as the rest of them. "I don't know if that would be a good idea."

She raised a brow and speared him with a look. "You said yourself they're after me. If they see me again, they'll come for me. Let them. It's your best bet to finding out who is helping the vampires and discovering what is being done."

"No," Court stated.

The same time Solomon said, "That could work."

Court looked askance at his eldest brother. "Have you lost your mind?"

"He knows it's the best way," Skye said.

Court looked at Myles for help, but Myles was looking at Skye as if she could be the answer for them. Court turned to Kane.

Kane threw up his hands. "Don't look at me. I don't think she should be out there either, but Solomon has the bit between his teeth now."

Court turned back to Skye. "Don't do this."

"I have to." She smiled up at him. "If I don't, they'll use whatever they're doing on an innocent. That blood will be on my hands because I could've stopped this and didn't."

"They would've used whatever this is regardless. You didn't start it," he argued.

"How do you know that?"

Court opened his mouth to dispute her question when he realized he had no ground to stand on. "You barely escaped last night with your life."

"I'll be fine if you're there."

Court looked into her eyes. Since the first moment he saw Skye, he felt the attraction. Strong. Undeniable. So far, he had been able to hold it at bay.

But with the way she was looking at him now, as if he alone could keep her alive, Court knew his ironclad control would shatter the first moment they were alone.

"What do you say?" Skye asked. "Will you help me?"

Court found himself nodding, even though he knew it was the worst idea they'd had in a long history of bad ideas. If Skye were taken...

He couldn't even finish the thought. She wasn't going to be taken.

Court slowly released a deep breath. "All right. But only with the condition that you do as I ask," he hurried to say when she smiled.

"Agreed," Skye said.

Myles lifted the phone receiver on his desk. "I'm going to call the NOPD. Perhaps our contact there can help turn the attention away from Skye in Matthew's murder."

"Good idea." Solomon slapped Court on the shoulder as he passed by. "Let's roll on this tonight. As soon as you have a plan, Court, we'll call another meeting."

Kane nodded to Skye and turned on his heel to follow Solomon out of the office. Court fidgeted. He looked at Myles to see his brother giving him a grin that said he knew exactly what Court was thinking – and feeling.

"What do I need to do?" Skye got to her feet and squared her shoulders. "I want to help, Court."

His gaze lowered to her lips. Full, dark pink lips. It was a mouth he pictured wrapping around his cock. He barely bit back a groan at the image that flashed in his head.

Those tempting lips parted slightly. Court jerked his eyes back up to her face, his blood heating when he saw the blatant interest reflected in her gaze.

Damn, he was in trouble.

"What happens when this is done?" he asked her.

A small frown appeared on her forehead. "What happens?"

"Yeah. Are you going to keep on exposing the supernatural? Are you going to expose me and my family?"

Her head nodded in understanding, but a furrow formed between her brows. "Oh. You think I would do that?"

"I think what my brother wants to know," Myles said, "is if your need to find answers will be satisfied."

Skye's dark gaze held Court's. "My roommate was killed by a vampire. I thought I knew how to protect myself. It's a truly horrific feeling to realize that I'm as unprepared and naïve as I was back in college." She paused to swallow. "I want a family one day. I want to be able to focus my worries on normal things like who my kids are texting and what they're watching on TV. I want to have my concern focused on their grades and teaching them the right things."

Court wasn't sure how he felt about the warmth that spread through him when she spoke of children. He could easily imagine her as a mother. She would look even more beautiful with her stomach swollen with child.

He halted his thoughts right there. What the

hell was wrong with him? Pregnant women weren't sexy.

No, but Skye sure as hell would be.

"You know what's out there. There's no going back from that." Court fisted his hands so he wouldn't reach out and touch her. "There are things you can do to protect yourself, your family, and your home. We can teach you that."

"After all I've done, you would do that?"

"Yes."

God, he would do so much more if she only asked.

Screwed. That's what he was. Royally, totally screwed.

Myles cleared his throat and got to his feet. "It might be better if you stayed here, Skye. Between the police and the vampires, no one will look for you here."

"Thank you," she said with a smile directed at Myles.

Court could have punched his brother. Her sweet and sexy smiles should only be directed at him. Certainly not at Myles, who was engaged to Addison.

Myles chuckled. Court shifted his gaze from Skye to his brother to see Myles looking at him. Court flipped him off. He didn't need anyone else noticing that he was becoming tangled in all that was Skye Parrish.

Addison poked her head around the door of Myles's office, her jaw-length blond hair drawing his brother's gaze. "Hey," she said with a smile full of love, happiness, and desire, all of it directed at Myles.

"Hey," Myles replied as he came around his desk. He held out his hand for her. "Come meet Skye."

Addison walked to Myles's side and wrapped an arm around him. She gave a welcoming smile to Skye as Myles did the introductions.

"Damn," Riley said when she came in. "You beat me to it, cuz," she said with a wink to Myles.

Myles laughed and pulled Addison close. "Skye, I think you'll find you fit in quite well here. Riley already thinks she runs things."

"Because I do," Riley interjected.

Addison rose up and kissed Myles. "Riley and I thought we'd take Skye off your hands for a bit. We can show her around."

"Show her around?" Court knew exactly what his cousin and soon-to-be sister-in-law were going to do. Talk. "The bar isn't that big."

Riley rammed her hip into his. Her sly smile said she also recognized his attraction to Skye. "Worried?"

"No," he mumbled. It was a lie, and they all knew it.

Skye grabbed her purse. "Show me the way, girls. Looks like I'll be here all day."

Court watched Skye walk out with Addison on one side of her and Riley on the other. He was glad Skye was making friends. Both the women would watch over her through the day. But he could do a better job.

"You got it bad, bro," Myles said as he walked up beside him.

"How screwed am I?"

Myles rubbed his chin. "One hundred percent. Don't bother fighting it. Just go for it."

CHAPTER EIGHT

Just go for it.

Those words reverberated in Court's head for the next four hours.

It was nice to look up from the bar to see Skye. She had put on one of the Gator Bait shirts and was waiting tables with Riley and Addison. Skye had said she couldn't stand to sit around, so she began to help the others out.

The more Court was around Skye, the more he found he liked. She might have originally caught his attention by the article in the paper. Her beauty might have kept his interest. But it was the warm, intelligent, friendly woman who drew him in deeper.

The lunch hour was busy, keeping him moving and filling drink orders. All the while, he kept running over scenarios in his head of how they could trap the vampires without using Skye. What irritated him was that they were going to have to use her. She might appear strong, but he saw the thread of fear she couldn't quite mask in those pretty eyes of hers.

That fear would help to keep her from doing something rash and reckless. At least he hoped it would. She had already done something careless by going to the Viper's Nest.

"A beer, please," came a deep voice behind him.

Court nodded as he finished making a martini. "Be right with you, bud." He put the garnish on the drink and turned around to find an NOPD detective sitting on a barstool.

It had been years since Scott Theriot was inside Gator Bait. Before Scott joined the police, he had been a regular at the bar. Such a regular that he and Court had become tight friends.

That friendship was strained when Scott had seen Court shift one night to save a woman and her child from a vampire. Scott wanted to know all about the LaRue curse after that.

Unfortunately, once Scott had learned everything, he stopped coming around. There were a few phone calls when Scott would want to know if a homicide he was investigating were supernaturally related or not. Other than that, nothing.

"Court," Scott said with a nod as he leaned his arms on the bar.

Court looked over his old friend's long and shaggy black hair and scruffy jaw in need of a shave. Scott's hazel gaze was cynical, distrustful.

"Detective," Court replied.

Scott looked around the bar. "You act surprised to see me. Myles left a message for me to come by. Said it had something to do with the murder last night."

Court looked down at the sink and the basin of water where he had been washing glasses. "Did he now?"

"Should I talk to Myles?"

"Up to you." Court poured Scott's beer and set it in front of him.

Scott blew out a breath. "Tell me what's going on."

"The murder last night wasn't done with a knife as it's being reported."

Scott lowered his gaze to the mug of beer. "I know. I didn't draw the case, but I had a look. Two small wounds on the victim's neck and all the blood gone. I know what that means."

"The woman your colleagues are looking for to question isn't involved. The victim accompanied her to a club but left without her. Kane and I had to save her from two vamps."

Scott shook his head, mumbling a string of curses. Then he looked back at Court. "Vamps means the Viper's Nest."

"Yep. They're after her. She's under our protection until we can get them off her trail. I don't trust anyone with her. She's found herself with a lot of enemies in a short time, and we know how well connected the supes are in town."

"You want me to keep the cops away from her?"

Court leaned his hands on the bar. "What we would appreciate is a heads up if NOPD decides to take a look here or any of our places. I don't know if the vamps want to kill her or turn her, but either way, they got her to leave the Viper's Nest without using their mind control."

That made Scott frown. "What?"

"They used some form of magic. We need to find out what it is, as well as who is teaming up with the vamps."

"I suppose you have a plan?"

Court nodded. "It'll involve returning to the Viper's Nest. We have to learn who is helping the vamps."

Scott turned his glass in a circle. "I saw what happened in the cemetery a few weeks back."

Court straightened. Why would Scott have been there? And why hadn't he shown himself?

"Y'all handled getting Myles's woman free well. None of the tourists, and most of the residents, didn't even know what was going on. Delphine almost got one over on you though."

"She won't ever stop." Court ran a hand down his face. "You should've let us know you were there."

Scott sat up and sighed loudly. He ran a hand through his hair and adjusted his faded red tee. "With all those weres and witches. I think not. The witch that was taken with Addison hasn't been seen since."

"She's fine," Court was quick to say. "Her coven turned on her so she decided to put some distance between them and her."

"Smart girl. Pretty, too."

Court shrugged. Minka was attractive, but she didn't compare to Skye.

Scott slid off the stool. "I can't promise anything, but I'll do my best."

He watched Scott walk out of the bar and into the bright sunlight. Court turned and found Riley beside him.

"He's cute," she said, watching until the door closed. Then she turned her gaze to Court. "Who was that?"

"Detective Scott Theriot."

"Really? How do you know him?"

"We used to be friends. Until he found out what I was."

Riley's face shifted into a frown. "What a jerk. None of us need friends like that."

"It scared him, Riley."

"I don't give a shit. He knew you, Court. He should've realized you never would have sharpened your teeth on his bones. Has he come here to make amends?"

Court grinned at his cousin, thankful for her words. "Myles called him about Skye. Scott said he would try to keep us informed if the cops turn this way."

"Right," Riley said with a roll of her eyes.

~ ~ ~

It had been years since Skye had waited tables, but it was something to occupy her time. Besides, she enjoyed Addison and Riley. The bar was much different than a restaurant, as well. It could be the music that made it such a good atmosphere to work in. It could be the place itself, or even the great food.

But she had a suspicion it had to do with a hunky blond werewolf with piercing blue eyes working behind the bar. Several times, Skye had looked up to find Court watching her.

It had been so long since she'd flirted with a guy that she was pretty rusty at it. Still, she wasn't going to let such an opportunity pass.

Court wasn't just breathtakingly gorgeous. He was focused on his family. She could see the man he was just by watching him with Riley, Addison, and his brothers. Court was a good guy. Even if there was a primal, dangerous vibe about him that made her heart race with excitement and a bit of fear.

Skye put on a brave face about returning to the vampire club. In truth, she wanted to be as far from it as she could get. The simple fact was, no matter how far she ran, the vampires would still be there.

She had created some enemies, and she never liked looking over her shoulder anyway. The only way she could get through the night was knowing that Court was there.

It still boggled her mind that she was surrounded by werewolves. Riley told her there was a pack that lived out in the swamps, as well. The Moonstone pack was once powerful in New Orleans, but they'd disappeared years ago. It was only recently that they had returned.

The only faction she hadn't met someone from was the Voodoo sect. Based on the story Addison had told her about Delphine, the Voodoo priestess who had taken it upon herself to rid the world of all Chiassons and LaRues, Skye had no interest in meeting her.

The stories hadn't stopped there. Riley had told Skye how Delphine had ventured to Lyons Point to terrorize her family on multiple occasions. Luckily, Riley's brothers and their women had come through it, each time defeating Delphine.

There was one story that was the hardest to hear, and that was Kane's. Myles had been the one to tell her about the laughing, friendly Kane, who rolled out of bed with messy hair and came to work.

But that was before Delphine had cursed him to kill the daughter of her enemy. When Delphine had sent Kane after Ava, she happened to be in Lyons Point. The curse prevented Kane from doing anything but hunting her. It became his singular purpose. Riley's brothers had protected Ava and stopped Kane.

But Kane hadn't been the same since. He was reserved, focused. He rarely smiled. His hair was always combed and his clothes were always neat and orderly.

That story explained so much about Kane that Skye forgave him immediately for all his harsh words. She immediately dispelled her nasty thoughts toward him.

"You've had a busy day."

Skye smiled as she recognized Court's voice. She set the dirty dishes down in the kitchen and turned to face him. "I have. It's been fun."

"Really?" he asked with a raised brow.

She shrugged. "Really. I'm not sure I'd want to do it all the time, but it kept my mind off things."

"I hear you've been told some of the recent happenings with our family."

"I have." She licked her lips. "Why haven't you killed Delphine?"

Court's chest expanded as he took a deep breath. "She's not easy to kill. We had the chance once."

"Why wouldn't you take it?" she asked, flabbergasted.

"We used the advantage to get her to remove the curse she put on Kane. If he would have killed anyone, whether it was Ava or not, he would've remained in wolf form for the rest of his life without knowing who he really was."

Skye was too shocked to speak for a moment. "I'd have done the same thing as you."

"I think it's time you took a break. Follow me."

He turned and walked from the kitchen. Skye hesitated, letting her gaze linger on his butt before she followed him. The guy could fill out a pair of jeans nicely. It didn't help that his shirt was tight enough to see every bulge and valley of his muscles. He must work out every day to have a body like that.

Skye found herself back in Myles's office again. Except this time, it was just her and Court. She looked around worriedly before she took one of the chairs.

Court sank into the one next to her. "I wanted to talk the plan over with you. If you're uncomfortable with any of it, we can change it."

"I should think the plan is fairly simple. You and I go to the club. You blend in, and I wait to be approached again. When I am, you rush in and take care of the nasties."

"Nasties?" he repeated with a choked laugh.

Skye lifted one shoulder in a shrug. "That's what my mother used to call monsters."

"It fits. Essentially, that is the plan. That's the basic version anyway. Riley and Addison will be there but outside the club. You're right. I'll be inside the club. We're known around town, so if more than one LaRue shows up, it'll make everyone wary."

She wasn't sure that was smart. Things could happen. Court could be outnumbered and they could attack him.

"They won't mess with me," Court said as if reading her mind. "It's not uncommon for one of us to visit the clubs to make sure everyone is obeying the rules."

Skye clasped her hands in her lap. "All right."

"Myles and Kane will be with the girls. Solomon will be hiding right outside the club, as well. If, for some reason, the vamps get you out before I can stop them, Solomon will be there."

She nodded. "Understood."

"You don't have to do this, you know."

She looked into his blue, blue eyes. "I do have to do this. For Jo, for myself, and for all the innocents out in the world. Besides, I need to set this right and get whatever enemies I've amassed off my butt."

"You can back out anytime," he urged.

"I'm doing this."

"Then you'll need to be prepared." Court handed her a silver knife.

CHAPTER NINE

It was wrong. Court knew it the moment he walked into the Viper's Nest. Now he wished he had waited to leave the bar after seeing Skye one more time. He sent off a text to his brothers so they would stop Skye from entering the club. No sooner had he hit send then the door opened and she walked in.

Court let out a string of curses. He glanced around, noting how a current went through the club. Everyone was looking at Skye. Some because they knew who she was. No doubt they also knew she had escaped from Jacques and Anton the previous night.

But many were eyeing her because of what she was wearing.

Court licked his lips. Her long hair was down, the curtain of black silk falling midway down her back. It was parted on the side, with one section tucked behind her ear.

She was once more in all black. The black pants emphasized her long legs while the black shirt dipped low to show off a wealth of creamy skin and cleavage.

Skye stood inside the club at the door for several seconds before she slowly walked to the bar in her black booties. The heels weren't nearly as tall as the previous night, but they were tall enough to cause him worry if she had to run.

Hell. Who was he kidding? Just thinking of her near a vamp was enough to cause him anxiety of the worst kind.

He watched as she placed a drink order and turned to watch the dance floor. The couples on the floor were half-naked, their bodies grinding against one another.

Her head turned slightly to the left where a vamp was drinking from a woman's neck as she stroked his cock. Skye quickly turned her head away.

Court's phone vibrated with a text. He looked down to see a reply from Myles asking if he was going to escort Skye out of the club. Court wanted nothing more, but he had a feeling Skye wouldn't leave easily.

He didn't want to make a scene of any kind. There were already too many vamps eyeing Skye as it was. Court waved on a scantily clad blond who was walking his way. She frowned but found a vampire soon enough.

Court spotted Anton making his way to him

and sent off a text to his brothers with just one number – 11. That was their signal that things were going to shit in a hurry.

"Well, well, well," Anton said loudly over the music as he stopped next to Court. "I didn't expect this."

Court swiveled his head as he felt someone on his other side and saw Jacques.

"Or that," Jacques said as he jerked his thumb over his shoulder toward Skye.

Court leaned back against the wall as casually as he could. It was one of the most difficult things he had ever done, especially when he wanted to kill both vampires right there. "You two broke the rules. Did you actually think we wouldn't check in on you?"

"Did you bring Skye as a gift?" Jacques asked.

"Touch her and you die." The words were out of Court's mouth before he could stop them.

Anton smiled deviously. "Has the youngest LaRue found himself a woman? Don't get too attached, wolf. I doubt she'll live long."

"Is that a threat?"

Anton glanced at Skye. "Fact."

"Do you know what she's doing?" Jacques asked. "She's writing articles about all of us. We vamps don't mind. The more, the merrier. But some...well, some don't like being pointed out so blatantly."

The Djinn. Court should've realized that sooner. The Djinn liked to keep themselves secret. They only showed themselves to their victims.

Unless you were in the supernatural world, no one even knew the Djinn were real. And they certainly weren't like I Dream of Jeannie.

They were pure evil, wicked to the extreme. They were malicious and cruel beyond words. They also loved to mess with humans to drive them mad and then torment them endlessly.

Skye had written an article on the Djinn recently. She described them to perfection, which meant she had seen one. That Djinn would want revenge.

But the Djinn hated vampires. They would never lower themselves to align with them.

Court realized he hadn't answered Jacques. "Yes, I know what Skye does for a living. Tourists come to this city to see the supernatural."

"Ah, but she's putting out the truth," Anton said. "We can't let that keep happening."

"So you want to kill her?"

Jacques laughed. "We never said we wanted to kill her."

Court felt sick to his stomach. It was just as he'd imagined. They wanted to turn her, to make her one of them.

"If she's one of us, she won't be writing any more articles," Anton stated.

Court saw two vampires slowly closing in on Skye from opposite ends of the bar. He tried to go to her, but Jacques put his hand on Court's shoulder.

"It'll be done quickly," the vampire said.

Court jerked away from Jacques. "What you

two are doing here gives me the right to kill you on the spot."

"You have no proof," Anton said.

Jacques rubbed his hands together. "But there was no way we wouldn't show up once we learned she was returning."

Court's vision turned red with rage. He shoved Jacques against the wall. "You're dead, vampire."

"Good luck with that," Jacques said and jerked his chin toward the bar.

Court's head swiveled toward Skye to see the two vampires nearly upon her. He could kill Jacques and Anton and hope that his brothers helped Skye, or he could go after Skye and find the vamps later.

He chose the latter option.

Court released Jacques and ran to Skye. Vampires came out of nowhere to block his path, shoving him and hitting him. His head was slammed into a table, and Court looked up through the blood dripping down his forehead and into his eyes.

Skye was looking at him wide-eyed with terror. Then she pulled the dagger out of her pocket and slashed at the vampire nearest her.

Court smiled when he heard the vampire scream in pain over the music. He fought against his attackers, his gaze constantly seeking Skye. One moment she was there, and the next she was fighting the vampires amid toppled tables and chairs.

He was glad he had given Skye the weapon. It

wouldn't do much damage, but it was enough to keep the vampires at bay until he got to her.

Court could no longer hold back his wolf. He shifted, shredding his clothes on a loud growl. With jaws snapping, he took bites out of several vampires, including Jacques before he broke free.

Court leapt atop a table and launched himself through the air to land on a vampire who had lunged at Skye. He latched onto the vampire's neck and clamped down hard, his teeth going through skin and muscle.

The vamp screamed and spun around, trying to dislodge Court. It wasn't until the door to the club was thrown open and his brothers walked in that Court released the vampire and landed beside Skye.

~ ~ ~

Skye was startled beyond words when she saw Court change into a werewolf. First his eyes glowed an inhuman yellow, then a ferocious growl sounded from him. His bones popped out of joint and fur sprouted along his skin as his clothes were ripped and fell to the floor.

It all happened in a matter of seconds, but it was burned into her memory for all eternity. She was so absorbed with watching Court that she forgot about her two attackers. They got too close. One tried to knock the knife from her hand, but she refused to be that weak.

She fought against them, ducking and spinning to stay out of their reach. They were fast though, super fast. Many times they guessed what she would do and were there before she twisted away.

Adrenaline kept her going, but she knew she wouldn't last long at this rate. And then Court was there, his teeth around the neck of a vampire.

Blood poured down the front of the vamp as Court clamped down harder. Skye slashed the vampire on her left and ducked when he tried to grab her.

The next thing she knew, Court was standing beside her. Her fingers itched to touch his tawny fur. He looked up at her with his yellow eyes, silently asking if she were all right.

She nodded, amazed at how huge he was. Court was easily twice the size of a normal wolf. He stood almost as tall as her chest, all danger and fury to anyone who looked her way.

The fighting had stopped in the club, but the music still played. Skye inched closer to Court as she looked up and saw Solomon, Myles, and Kane standing at the door.

By the way their eyes flashed yellow, they too were ready to shift and take on some vampires.

Court put his head under her hand and took a step. Skye understood. She walked with him to the door as his lips peeled back to show his sharp teeth and he issued a low, rumbling growl to the vampires.

As soon as Skye was out of the club, Solomon wrapped an arm around her. "You're all right now."

"They knew I would be there," she said.

Solomon didn't stop walking. He hurried her away from the Viper's Nest with Myles on her other side. Kane was behind them, and Court loped ahead.

"They didn't get you," Myles said. "Focus on that."

Skye looked down at her hand that still held the knife. It was because of Court. He had been there, but the vampires prevented him from getting to her. If she hadn't had the knife, they would have gotten her.

By the time Gator Bait came into view, Court veered off to the left with Kane following him. Solomon and Myles ushered her around the back of the bar and through the kitchen to Myles's office. Addison and Riley were already there.

"She's in shock," Addison told Myles.

Riley put a glass in Skye's hand. "Drink this. All of it. Now."

Skye didn't look at what was inside. She tossed back the contents and swallowed. Then she spent the next few moments coughing as the bourbon burned its way down her throat.

"Now look at me," Riley said as she leaned over to look into Skye's face. "How do you feel?"

Images of the hissing vampires hitting Court with their fangs out flashed in her mind.

"Skye?"

She blinked as she recognized Court's voice. He was kneeling in front of her. As she looked into his face, she'd never felt so relieved in her life. She threw her arms around his neck and held him.

His arms enfolded her in a fierce hug. "It's all right. You did good."

"They knew I would be there," she repeated.

Court leaned back and cupped his hands around her face. "I know."

"I'll clean the blade," Kane said and tried to take the knife from her.

Skye pulled her hand away, daring him to reach for it again.

Kane smiled. "I'll return it to you."

The night had gotten to her in ways she hadn't known were possible. She knew a few basic moves to fend off an attacker that she'd learned through a website, but she had never been tested like she was tonight.

She breathed through her mouth as she grew nauseous. Skye handed the knife to Kane.

"She's losing color," Riley said.

Skye was soon wrapped in a blanket. She didn't understand why until she started to shiver. That's when she recognized that Riley was right. She was in shock. She knew because she'd experienced it one other time in her life.

Court adjusted the blanket and gave her a comforting smile.

How could he do that after what had happened? How could he pretend that someone hadn't betrayed him?

"Who else knew we would be there?" she asked.

Court sighed. "An old friend."

CHAPTER TEN

Court was livid. The anger was boiling over, souring his stomach like acid. Of all the people who might betray him, he'd never counted Scott as one of them.

Now he knew the truth.

Skye's dark gaze watched him with confusion and worry. He hated that she was more anxious than when she'd left the bar earlier. Tonight was supposed to make her safe from the vamps once and for all. At least that's what he had hoped for.

"Scott," Myles said with clenched teeth.

Court rubbed Skye's arms through the blanket. He didn't want to talk about it in front of her. She was still in shock. And he was still getting over seeing her surrounded by vampires.

He didn't like the helpless feeling he'd had

when the vampires had prevented him from getting to Skye. In all the times he'd shifted, not once had he felt so...savage.

Skye lowered her gaze. Was she scared of him now? Was the shock wearing off as she remembered what she had seen him do? Court dropped his arms and stood, staring at the top of her dark head.

He prayed she wasn't afraid of him. Skye was brave and courageous. If she feared him...

Court refused to finish the thought. He raised his gaze to find his brothers, Addison, and Riley staring at him. It suddenly felt as if he were a lab rat being studied.

"What happened in there?" Riley asked. "As soon as you sent the text, Addison and I came back here."

Court ran a hand through his hair. He was wired after shifting and battling the vampires. It didn't help that he craved the feel of Skye's body like his wolf yearned to run.

He leaned back against Myles's desk. "Jacques and Anton came up on either side of me. I assumed they wanted to give me shit about the previous night, but they were too interested in Skye. I knew every vamp in there was focused on her, but I didn't realize how much until it was too late."

Court closed his eyes as he recalled the fear that had spiked through him when he saw the vampires closing in on Skye. He took a deep breath and opened his eyes. "I saw them moving towards Skye, and I tried to get to her."

"But they stopped him," Skye said with a little tremor in her voice.

Court shifted his gaze to her. She was no longer hunched over, but rather sitting straight in the chair. Beautiful and brave.

Her eyes lifted to look at the others. "They were beating him, kicking him. I had no time to get out with the vampires blocking my way. Then they were on me."

"I shifted," Court said, picking up where Skye left off. "And began attacking. Skye fended off the vampires with the knife until I could get to her. That's when y'all came in."

Kane snorted. "This could've gone very badly."

"Operative word is could've," Solomon said. "It didn't."

Myles grabbed Addison's hand. "How desperately do they want Skye, Court?"

"They'll continue to come after her."

Myles's lips thinned. "That's what I thought. Skye, you realize you can't go home, right?"

"I do," Skye said and lifted her chin.

Solomon crossed his arms over his chest. "Court's place is out. It's the second stop they'll make after Skye's since he was with her inside the club. That leaves Kane's apartment or my house."

"The LaRue house." Riley shrugged when Kane looked at her. "I'm thinking how tiny your apartment is. There is plenty of room at Solomon's. Besides, it's outside the city so we can keep the battle from overflowing into the streets."

Myles winked at her. "I agree with Riley."

"Then we need to get to my place," Solomon said.

Court glanced at the clock on the wall. "They'll be watching the bar. Getting Skye out is going to be difficult."

"Not too difficult," Kane said as he pulled out his phone and dialed a number.

Skye looked from Kane to Court. "Who is he calling?"

"More weres." He watched her carefully to see how she would react to that news.

"Oh," she mumbled.

Other than that one word, she didn't so much as twitch a muscle. Perhaps she wasn't as afraid as he thought. Then again, she had never seen him shift before. For those unaccustomed to such things, it could be very frightening.

A moment later, Kane ended the call and nodded. "Griffin and the Moonstone pack will be here shortly."

"Marcus can lock up the bar," Myles said.

Kane looked at Riley. "You stay beside me. If the vampires can't get Skye, they'll take anyone they can get."

"That goes for you, too," Myles said to Addison.

Skye shifted nervously in her chair, drawing Court's attention. Getting her out of the city and to the house he grew up in was going to be dangerous. But so was staying at the bar.

The LaRues were generally left alone, but the

vampires wanted Skye because of her articles. It was time to remind the vampires – and all the factions – who the LaRues were.

Court pushed away from the desk and walked out of the office. He wanted to confront Scott, but it would only end with his jaws around the detective's throat. He wouldn't be able to control his anger. The last thing the LaRues needed was the police at their door because one of their own was dead.

He slammed his hand into the back door in the kitchen and stepped out into the night air. The humidity was thick, the threat of rain hanging heavy in the air. September was prime time for hurricanes. That's all they needed on top of the chaos.

"Talk to me, Court," Solomon said from behind him.

Court clenched his hands into fists. He wanted to be alone. He didn't want or need any of his brothers worrying about him. Ever since their parents were murdered by Delphine and her people, Solomon and Myles had tried to protect him and Kane.

"I'm an adult, Solomon. I can handle this."

"The great thing about family, kid, is that you don't have to. We're here to help. Let us. Scott might have been your friend, but Myles is the one who called him."

Court hung his head, keeping his back to his eldest brother. "She could've been taken. God, you have no idea how close they came."

"I saw the bloody mess you made in the Viper's Nest. With us, words aren't always needed. You got to her, Court. She's safe."

"For now."

Solomon sighed audibly. "I know you like her. I'll do everything I can to ensure you don't have to endure what I did."

Court squeezed his eyes closed. Perhaps there would come a time when Solomon no longer felt the pain of loss from the murder of his woman. It had been years, but the violent death had shaken the brothers as nothing since their parents' murder had.

"She was your fiancée, Solomon. That's a bit different than me desiring Skye."

There was a pregnant pause. "The sooner we get to the house the better. Griffin and his pack will be here soon. I need you ready."

"I am," Court bit out.

"No, you're angry. You need to push that aside. The only way Skye is going to get through this is if you have your head on straight. We'll deal with Scott and his betrayal afterward."

Court lifted his head and faced his brother. "Apparently, the vamps need to be reminded who is keeping the peace around here."

"Agreed." Solomon's eyes flashed yellow. "I'm more than ready to pay the Viper's Nest a visit and deliver some justice. But not until we know for certain who is working with the vampires."

"I've never felt so...powerless. It's a new emotion, and frankly, I fucking hate it."

Solomon's gaze lowered to the ground. "You prepared Skye with a weapon. That's more than I did for my woman. We're werewolves, Court, not superheroes."

"Almost the same damn thing. The vampires used a coordinated attack, Solomon. It worked, sort of. They'll use it again."

Solomon's blue gaze lifted to meet Court's. "I'm counting on it."

Court watched his brother walk back inside the bar. Each of them had dated, but nothing lasted longer than six months. Solomon was the one who didn't shy away from love. He shouldered the most out of all of them, and it wasn't fair that he'd had his happiness ripped from his arms.

With a glance at the sky, Court returned to the bar. He paused, nodding to Marcus and the other cook as they worked the tickets.

Marcus knew what the LaRues were. He'd known ever since Solomon had saved him years ago. If anyone could keep the bar safe while they were out, it was Marcus.

Court walked through the kitchen. He glanced out into the bar and spotted Gage, Griffin's brother, sitting with another Moonstone were, Jaxon.

It was time.

Court made his way to the office. He stopped in the doorway when he saw Skye talking to Riley. Skye turned to him, her dark eyes meeting his.

"Ready?" he asked.

"No."

He could understand that. But if they were going to have any sort of chance, Skye had to be on board all the way. Court walked to her and squatted beside her chair.

"I never intended for you to see me shift-"

"I know," she said quickly, looking down at her hands.

Court sighed. She was afraid of him.

"Riley will stay beside you," Court said, glancing at his cousin.

Skye's forehead puckered in a frown as her gaze snapped back to his face. "Where will you be?"

"I'll be near."

Riley rose from the chair. "I think you should be the one with Skye. I've been ordered to stay next to Kane anyway."

"Whatever works," Skye said.

Court would feel better if he was beside her, but he didn't want her any more afraid of him than she already was. "Is there anything you need?"

"My knife."

Kane walked in, followed by Griffin. "It's here, Skye." He handed her the weapon, and she tucked it back in her pocket.

Court stood and motioned to Griffin. "Skye, this is Griffin, head of the Moonstone clan. He's a friend."

She gifted Griffin with a half-smile as she climbed to her feet.

Court watched Griffin's green eyes look Skye over appreciatively. When Griffin turned his gaze to him, Court was using all of his control not to bash the wolf's face in.

Griffin merely smiled before nodding his head of dark brown hair to Skye. "Nice to meet you, ma'am. Kane told me you're in a spot of trouble. My people and I will be happy to help."

"Thank you," Skye said and moved closer to Court.

It helped to tamp down some of his anger, but the more Griffin looked at her, the worse it became.

Griffin laughed and slapped Court on the shoulder. "No need to worry."

"Let's get moving," Myles said as he strode into the office. He grabbed Addison's hand and walked back out.

Kane motioned Riley out with Griffin following them.

Court looked down at Skye. She squared her shoulders and walked out of the office. He waited a moment, watching her before he followed. Behind him was Solomon.

"What's the plan?" Skye asked over her shoulder.

Court put his hand on her back and ushered her through the kitchen and out the back door. "We leave as one. Griffin will stay with us while his wolves set up a wider circle."

"You have a vehicle that will fit all of us?"

Solomon chuckled as he let the bar door close behind him. "We're walking."

Skye's eyes widened. "Isn't that going to give them ample opportunity to attack?"

Court nodded as Griffin walked out of the small fenced-in area at the back of the bar. "Probably."

CHAPTER ELEVEN

Probably? Had he just said probably? Skye wasn't so sure she was up for this. Matter of fact, she was certain of it.

She was unceremoniously – but gently – pushed through the gate by Court. His large hand was warm through her clothes, steady. He thought she had courage, which was the only thing that kept her legs moving. If he knew the truth – that she was the biggest scaredy cat around – his opinion would change drastically.

But she wasn't going to tell him. She wanted him to think she was courageous and bold for as long as she could. Eventually, he would learn the truth.

Her legs felt wooden, and her stomach still rolled from the adrenaline dump earlier. The bourbon Riley had kept feeding her was helping. Otherwise, she would still be sitting in the office with the blanket as a shield.

"Oh, God," she muttered beneath her breath as they walked farther from the bar.

Every shadow, every sound was a potential attack. Skye was completely reevaluating her love of horror movies. If she survived the night, she was never eagerly watching Freddy Kruger again.

She glanced at Court. He was stoic, solid. Tough. He didn't appear fazed by the night at all.

Except for when he'd shifted and tore through the vampires.

Skye shivered as she recalled those few seconds that had felt like months. Afterward, she'd made a complete fool of herself and threw her arms around him, just thankful that he was alive.

"Are you afraid of me now?" Court asked in a low voice as they walked.

Skye frowned. Afraid of him? Where did he get that idea? "Why would you think that?"

"You won't look at me."

She turned her head to him and gaped. Court grabbed her and moved her out of the way of an oncoming group of people. On her other side, Griffin chuckled.

"No, I'm not afraid of you," she answered and looked forward.

She could feel him watching her. He was a force unto himself, and she didn't even think he realized it. It was obvious as they walked down the sidewalk with Griffin a little ahead of her. Anytime someone got too near her, Court pulled her toward him.

Most took one look at his stern face and gave them a wide berth.

"I never intended to shift in front of you," he finally said.

Skye shook her head in confusion. "Why? It's part of who you are."

"You're freaked enough already with the vampires. Why would I want to scare you more?"

"I like to know what I'm dealing with."

He made a sound at the back of his throat. "Are you telling me that you're not a little uneasy about the fact that so many weres are around?"

"What makes me nervous is the fact there are vampires after me," she said tightly.

Griffin glanced over his shoulder at her and gave her a nod of approval. Strangely, that made her feel better.

They grew quiet as they continued through the city until they reached the outskirts and the sidewalks ended. All around her were huge live oaks with their branches stretching outward, some so heavy they rested on the ground.

Skye thought the city was scary, but it was nothing compared to the woods. Just the thought of it made her shake. Her eyes were wide, her heart pounding in her ears. Vampires were fast. Really fast.

But so was Court. She hadn't expected that of a werewolf. Or the sheer size of him.

He laced his fingers with her cold ones. Skye

looked at him, thankful he was beside her.

"How much farther?" she asked.

Court's face was half hidden in the night, but she could still see his anxiety. "Too damn far."

The cicadas were loud, their music surrounding them like a symphony. Above them, the occasional bat in its frenzied flight to catch mosquitos appeared. Skye was busy keeping the nasty insects from biting. How she hated when they buzzed near her ear.

She slapped at her arm, killing a mosquito. An owl hooted twice. The cicadas gave a crescendo of noise before the sound died to nothing for a few seconds.

Griffin slowed until he came even with Skye. He looked over her head to Court and said in a low voice, "I expected something by now."

"We all did," Court whispered.

Skye was just happy that nothing had happened so far.

They moved off the road through the woods. Every moment became scarier than the last. Skye saw multiple opportunities for a vampire to attack or a place for them to hide. She really didn't know how much more stress she could handle before her heart just gave out.

Court never loosened his hold on her hand. Being flanked by two werewolves was comforting. It was a thought she'd never imagined herself having.

For so long, she thought the only good people in the supernatural world were the witches. Not because she'd had a bad experience with demons, werewolves, or Djinn, but because she assumed they were all evil.

She was learning she had been wrong about a great many things. The one thing that hadn't changed was the knowledge that vampires were nasty, vile creatures.

The group seemed to walk forever on a trail that apparently only the werewolves could see. What little light the moon shed was barely enough to keep Skye from stepping on anything. What she wouldn't give for a flashlight. Or a car.

Practical shoes.

Mosquito spray.

The LaRue house.

Court halted, jerking her against him before spinning her away and shoving her at Griffin. Skye's heart leapt into her throat as she waited to see a vampire, but nothing jumped out into the night. She looked over to find Court bending before grabbing something from the ground. Her mouth fell open when she realized he had a snake by its tail before snapping it like a whip, breaking its neck instantly.

"That was a cottonmouth," Griffin whispered. "One of the only snakes that won't run from humans. They're aggressive."

Court held out his hand after he tossed the snake away, and Skye eagerly went to him. Now she wasn't just scared of vampires. There were snakes out there that were hostile, too.

This night just kept getting better and better.

It felt like an eternity before she saw a structure through the trees. It didn't take her long to realize it was a house.

They came out of the trees to a grand area of nothing but grass. In the middle sat a stately home. It's tall columns and wrap-around porch were indicative of plantation homes in the south.

Court made her stay back as Solomon and several of Griffin's men walked in and around the house to make sure it was safe. As soon as Solomon waved them in, Court ran, pulling her with him.

Skye let out a relieved breath as soon as she was inside. She bent over, her hands on her knees as she drug in deep breaths.

She straightened while the others set up in different rooms with a clear view out the windows. Skye glanced through the narrow pane of glass next to the door and saw many of the Moonstone pack setting up a patrol around the perimeter of the house.

Court placed his hand on her back and turned her away from the door. "Are you hungry? Thirsty? Do you need anything?"

She could only shake her head, her eyes darting in each room as he hurried her past them. She had no time to notice anything about the house other than the very wide foyer she was walking through.

Then she was at the stairs. Court led her up them, turning her left, and not stopping until he reached the second door. He opened it and walked inside.

Skye paused a moment before she followed him in. Court clicked on a light, flooding the room. It was a good-sized bedroom with a black wrought iron bed against the far wall. There was an old, dark wood desk with many dings and scratches on the wall closest to Skye.

She looked up at Court, watching as he looked around the room as if remembering. That's when she knew. "This is your bedroom."

"It was." His chest constricted as he drew in a breath. "The house is warded against any enemy we might have. Nothing will get through the doors."

"Wow." She didn't know what else to say. She hadn't even known those kinds of wards were possible.

Court ran a hand down his face. "It's been a long night. You should try to rest."

Right. As if that were going to happen.

Skye walked deeper into the room and sat on the bed. "Why didn't the vampires attack?"

"I don't know, but it worries me."

"Do they know they can't get to us here?"

Court nodded slowly. "They do. Which makes it even more troublesome."

"Maybe they've given up trying to get to me," she said hopefully.

One side of his mouth kicked up in a grin. "I sincerely hope so, but in my experience with vamps, they don't give up easily."

She glanced down at her hands. "You know, I meant it earlier. I'm not afraid of you."

"I saw your face, Skye."

"I wasn't prepared to see a werewolf, but whatever fear I might have had vanished because you were protecting me. That kinda changes a girl's view."

Court's bright blue eyes watched her for long, silent moments. "You're one of a kind."

"Hardly," she said with a snort. "I'm stubborn, and I don't think things through all the way, which gets me in trouble."

"You're fearless."

"No."

He moved away from the open door across the room and sat beside her. "I've known people who thought they could handle anything. They claimed to be brave, but at the first sign of true and imminent danger, they ran away. You didn't."

"I didn't have a choice," she argued.

"You did." Court turned his head to her and smiled. "You made the choice to go back into the Viper's Nest. You made the choice to stay with us. You made the choice to leave the bar and come here."

He made her sound so...valiant. It warmed her.

She returned his grin. "I wish I could take credit, but I was following your lead."

"Which shows how smart you are," he said with a wink.

Their shoulders were touching, their gazes locked. Skye was drowning in the depths of his blue eyes. Chills raced over her skin from being so close to him.

They had held hands for the past hour, but

being so close to him now while they were alone, wasn't just comforting. It was heady.

Sexual tension sparked between them as their smiles faded. Her stomach fluttered when his gaze lowered to her mouth. She held her breath when he leaned toward her.

She slowly moved to him, anxious to kiss him. Then they were interrupted by a knock at the door.

CHAPTER TWELVE

Court jerked his head to the door, ready to take someone's head off when he saw Solomon. He stood and nodded to his brother. "How's it looking?"

"Quiet. Too quiet." Solomon leaned against the door jam and looked at Skye. "How are you doing?"

Skye smoothed a hand down her hair. "Much better now that I'm here."

"Make yourself at home. I'm not sure how long you'll be staying," Solomon said.

It was something Court had intentionally left out. He'd been afraid if he told Skye she might be at the house for several days, she might not have come. Then again, she wanted to live. She seemed to understand that her best chance to do that was with them.

Skye's eyes widened. She turned her gaze to Court. "How long am I going to have to wait?"

"That's hard to say. We don't know exactly who is working with the vampires, which means it's still not safe for you to go out during the day."

Solomon shrugged. "It's your decision, Skye. You can either stay here and trust us to help you or you can leave."

"If I leave, I won't have your protection. Is that what you're saying?"

Court was about to correct her when Solomon gave him a quick look to silence him.

"That's right," Solomon said. "A lot of people willingly put themselves out there tonight to get you here. You really don't want to waste their efforts, do you?"

Skye slowly let out a long breath. She looked at the floor. "No."

"Good. Get some rest," Solomon said and pulled Court out of the room as he closed the door behind him.

Court opened his mouth, but Solomon turned him around and gave him a shove. Court had no choice but to walk down the hallway and descend the stairs.

When he landed in the foyer, he whirled around. "Why did you lie to her?"

"Do you really need to ask?" Solomon said as he reached the bottom. "If she leaves, the vamps will find her and turn her. Is that what you want."

"You know it isn't."

"Then I did what had to be done."

Court briefly squeezed his eyes closed. "Even if she changes her mind and leaves, I'm going to protect her."

"As we all will, but I'm trying to save us that trouble. It's easier to fight here."

Court knew that was the truth, but he still didn't like lying to Skye. She didn't deserve that. The only thing that kept him from running back up the stairs and telling her was the memory of Solomon holding Misty's dead body in his arms.

Solomon walked away, leaving Court standing there trying to come to terms with what was going on. It never entered his mind to fight the attraction he felt for Skye. It had been there from the first time he'd seen her, but the fire had grown the more they were together.

It was a good thing Solomon interrupted them before that kiss because Court wasn't so sure he could've stopped once he'd gotten a taste of her sweet lips.

"She'll be all right," Myles said as he came to stand by him.

Court looked up the stairs. "I sincerely hope so."

~ ~ ~

Five days. Five very long days.

Skye loved the old house, as well as Riley and Addison's company, but the situation was draining and grating on her nerves. In order to get some time alone, she had closed herself up in her room and wrote the article on her phone.

Typing a text was one thing. Typing an article on her phone was the worst type of torture. Especially with the stupid auto-correct that always changed the wrong words and left misspelled ones.

She didn't tell Court or the others that she was writing it. Skye had a deadline to meet and had promised the article, so she had to write it.

That was three days ago. The article would be up today. She was nervous about it. Mostly, however, she was worried about how the brothers would feel about what she had written.

"It's your turn," Riley said as they sat around the gaming table.

Skye blinked and focused on her hand of cards. They had been playing Spades for the past two hours. She glanced down at the cards that had been played and chose the ten of clubs. She couldn't win the hand, and it was her largest club card.

Minka let out a little whoop and collected the cards, winning the trick. "I'm smoking y'all," she said and tossed down the queen of clubs.

"When are the boys getting back?" Addison asked as she placed a two of clubs.

Riley shrugged, a smirk on her face as she laid the ace of clubs on top of the others. "Any moment."

"Oh, you sneak!" Minka said, laughing.

Skye laughed as she threw down the seven of clubs, giving Riley the win.

Minka rolled her eyes at the look Addison kept

giving her. "Stop it. I don't care what Solomon has to say. He can kiss my sweet ass if he doesn't like me here."

"Amen," Riley said with a wink.

Skye took a long drink of her sweet tea. "What is it with Solomon. Why doesn't he like you? You saved Myles from death when he had all that silver in his system."

"I don't know," Minka said with a shrug. "Some people just rub each other wrong. That's us, I suppose. I don't care enough to even worry about it."

But Skye knew that for the lie it was. She hadn't been around very long, but it was obvious from the tightening of Minka's body every time Solomon's name was brought up that she very much cared what the eldest LaRue thought of her.

They played the next round, ribbing each other. Addison thought she was going to win since she had the ace of diamonds, but Skye didn't have any diamonds, so she played a spade, winning the trick.

Skye calmly pulled the cards her way with a smile and a little dance in her chair.

"Oooooh. You got whooped," Riley told Addison.

Minka covered her mouth with her cards, her eyes playfully wide as she looked at Addison. She lowered the cards. "Looks like we need to watch this one."

Addison lifted her nose and fought to keep the smile from her face as she pretended to be affronted. Then she burst out laughing.

It felt good to be a little normal in such a strange situation. Skye knew Riley, Addison, and even Minka were doing their best to keep her mind off things. However, she wasn't sure how much longer she could stay at the LaRue house.

There was the sound of talking from the front porch. Skye recognized Court's voice. She sat up in her chair, hoping that he'd found something during his patrol of the land around the home.

He was the first one in the house. His tall, muscular form filling the parlor entry. With his windblown blond hair, she knew he had been running. The fact his clothes were spotless told her he had been in wolf form.

"Hey," he said, his gaze going to her.

Her heart leapt and she couldn't help but smile when his blue eyes landed on her. He didn't look at anyone else, and it made her stomach feel as if there were butterflies taking off. "Hey. Good news?"

"No news," he said as he moved over to make room for Myles to walk past as he went to Addison and kissed her.

Skye wished Court would kiss her. It was all she'd thought about for five days since they'd almost kissed in his room.

"Nothing?" Addison asked.

Solomon stopped next to Court in the doorway. His gaze instantly went to Minka, who sat with her back to him. Minka was looking at her cards as if she didn't have a care in the world.

"What are you doing here?" Solomon asked.

He didn't say Minka's name, nor did he have to. She knew he was talking to her. Skye could've kicked him because the little burst of excitement on Minka's face vanished instantly, her hackles rising.

Minka played her next card and said, with her voice dripping with sarcasm, "So good to see you too, Solomon. No, I don't have anything to share, but I'm so glad you asked."

Skye watched as Court elbowed Solomon in the side before motioning his head to Minka.

Solomon rolled his eyes dramatically. "Of course, you're welcome in the house, Minka. We would appreciate anything you can add to help."

He said the words tightly, as if each syllable was painful to get past his lips.

"Of course," Minka replied silkily.

Skye set the rest of her cards face down on the table. "Still nothing? I don't understand."

"We don't either." Court ran a hand through his hair. "There are no tracks out there other than ours."

"This makes no sense," Riley said. "If the vamps want her, and they know she's here, why haven't they attacked? Or at least tried."

Minka lifted her eyes to Skye. "They're waiting on something."

That's when it hit Skye. A small tremor raced down her back. "They're waiting for me to leave."

Minka nodded slowly. "They have all the time in the world. They know you'll eventually think you're safe and return home."

"Not going to happen," Court stated.

Skye glanced at him. Minka was right. She was getting lax. With every day that passed without vampires or other supernatural creatures attacking, she began to think she had imagined it all.

"I can't stay here forever. Nor will the Moonstone clan remain," Skye said.

Court shook his head. "I know what you're thinking. The answer is no. We already put you out there once. Not. Happening."

"I can't live like this, and neither can any of you. I will never be able to repay what any of you have done for me, but we all know we'll have to make a decision soon."

Myles rested his hands on Addison's shoulders as he stood behind her chair. "I hate to agree, but Skye's right."

"The vamps knew we would retreat here," Riley said and flatted her lips. "Man, I hate those assholes."

"It's not just the vampires," Minka pointed out.

That was the kicker. They had no idea which one of the factions was helping the vampires. Magic was being used, but that could be the Djinn, witches, or even Delphine.

"Give me another few days," Court asked Skye. "Please."

She nodded, unable to tell him no. He turned on his heel and walked out of the house. She tracked him through the window in the parlor until he was out of sight.

"If there's anything to find, Court will find it," Myles said.

Skye slid her gaze to him and forced a smile. "I think you're right."

"You mean a lot to him," Solomon said.

Skye's heart missed a beat. The very idea that that could be true made her extremely happy. She looked at him. "Why do you say that?"

"He's proving it to you every day, Skye," Solomon said as he leaned against the doorway. "He patrols all night, only catching little naps when we make him take a break. He's hardly eaten in days. Like all of us, he knows the attack is coming, and he wants to make sure there are no surprises."

"Which will happen if I leave."

Solomon nodded his head once.

Skye looked at each person in the room. "There has to be something we can do to get this attack over with. If we wait too long, we won't have the other weres for help."

"She's right," Kane said as he walked into the room. "They're already getting antsy. Griffin is keeping them here for now."

Minka leaned forward and propped her elbows on the table. "I didn't come just to play cards, Skye. I came here because I have an idea. One that I think could get you out of this mess."

"Took you long enough," Solomon mumbled.

Skye watched the two of them, wondering if Solomon disliked Minka as much as he put on. Or if there were something more there. Skye was beginning to think there was something more.

CHAPTER THIRTEEN

Court stood back by a stand of trees and stared at the house he'd grown up in. There were many good memories there, but it was the night their parents were murdered that always came to mind when he looked at it.

He loved coming home, but it was hard. Their family had been shattered in one night because of a vengeful Voodoo priestess who didn't want the five factions to have any type of peace.

Delphine had gotten her wish with his parents' deaths. Now she needed to die. If she wasn't causing problems with the LaRues, she was messing with the Chiassons. So far, neither family had lost another member to Delphine's attempts.

But how long could their luck hold out.

Then there was Skye.

Court blew out a deep breath. The woman was constantly on his mind. He thought about her even in sleep. Her laugh, her lips turning up in a sensual smile, her long black hair, her smoky eyes. Her body.

She drove him mad with desire. He craved her, yearned for her. Burned for her.

Being around her so much over the past days had been the sweetest kind of torture. He would find ways to get as close to her as he dared. Occasionally, he'd let their hands brush. He even sunk so low as to touch her hair when she passed. Each time he returned from a patrol, he fought not to go to her, to pull her into his arms for a kiss as Myles did Addison.

Court grew hard just picturing Skye in his arms, imagined kissing her slowly, seductively, passionately. It was why he chose to patrol all night, because he couldn't be in the same house as her and not go to her.

He wasn't fighting it. He wanted to go to Skye. Court knew making love to her would be amazing. But she was being hunted by the vamps. He had to concentrate on that threat.

There was a slight movement to his left. Court shifted his gaze and saw Kane walk silently around a tree. Kane came to stand beside him, and for long moments, neither brother said a word.

"How many more nights are you going to spend out here watching the house?" Kane asked.

Court took immediate offense. "I patrol."

"In between staring at the house and thinking

of Skye."

Court didn't bother to deny it. But he didn't want to talk about it either. "How long to do you think Riley will stay?"

"As long as she needs to."

"She's done you good."

Kane lifted one shoulder in a half-shrug. "Riley is a strong woman. She's a Chiasson. But she also needed someone. She's not as happy as she makes out."

That made Court frown. "Is it her brothers?"

"I don't know. I don't ask questions."

"Which is apparently exactly what she needs."

"Yeah," Kane mumbled. After a long stretch of silence, he said, "I don't know if we would've acted any differently than our cousins if we'd had a sister."

Court grunted. "I've thought the same thing. Riley is hurt by their actions, but it's done out of love. They want to protect her."

"I think she believes they think her weak."

"Riley?" Court asked as he swiveled his head to Kane. "Weak? Not possible."

Kane raised a brow as one side of his lips lifted in a sort of smile. "I know. But Vincent, Lincoln, Beau, and Christian might have forgotten her strength while Riley was away at college."

"I'm glad she came here. Even with the danger, it's good to make that connection with our cousins again."

Kane turned so that he faced Court. "There's another connection that needs to be made. Get your ass in the house and kiss Skye like you've been longing to do."

Court blinked, taken aback. "What?"

"I know you, Court. The fact you've kept your distance from Skye tells me how much you like her."

Was it that obvious? Did the others know, as well? Did he care that they knew? No, he realized, he didn't.

"I do like her," he admitted. "I don't want to screw it up."

"Then go see her," Kane said and gave him a little push. "We've got things covered out here."

Once his feet started moving, Court couldn't stop. He walked to the house, up the steps to the porch, and through the front door. He paused long enough to close the door softly behind him, listening for Skye.

Court walked to the kitchen, glancing inside rooms as he went. He found Minka sitting alone at the kitchen table with a glass of untouched bourbon in her hand.

"She's in her room," Minka said with a smile.

Court nodded to the bottle. "Do you not like the brand?"

"I'm just thinking."

"You didn't have to come, but I'm glad you did. I'm sorry Solomon is such an ass."

Minka waved away his words. "I can handle Solomon. I'm more concerned with the plan."

He was too, but Court wasn't going to add more worry to her. "How did you know I was looking for Skye?"

At this, Minka chuckled. "You can't seriously be asking me that question with the way you've been looking at her."

"I guess not," Court said with a smile.

He walked to the fridge and got out two longneck beers. He waved goodnight to Minka and headed up the stairs. When he was outside his old bedroom door, he stopped and knocked.

A moment later, the door opened. Court held up the beers and smiled. "Care for a refreshment?"

"I'd love one," Skye said as she stepped aside and opened the door wider for him.

He walked into his bedroom and looked around at how she had made it hers. There were piles of clothes off in the corner. Her things that he had gotten for her four days earlier from her place.

Court cleared his throat and pulled his gaze away from the laundry and the memory of being inside her house and looking through her belongings.

He turned and set the bottles on the desk, twisting off first one cap and then the other. Then he held one out for her. Their fingers brushed as she took the offered beer.

Their eyes held for a moment before she leaned against the wall. Court remained across from her and propped his shoulder against the opposite wall.

"I'm surprised you aren't on patrol," she said into the silence.

He shrugged. "I wanted to give Myles time with Addison."

"I hate that everyone is doing all of this because of me. I'm a nobody, Court. Why should any of you care if I'm taken?"

He couldn't believe the thought had even entered her head. "Why do you say that?"

"I have no family, no friends, really. There's no one who would even miss me if I died."

"I would."

Her dark gaze locked with his. "You don't know me."

"I do. I know you're funny, brave, stubborn, and relentless. I know you value friendship and responsibility. I know you want to protect the innocent as we do."

"That's not all there is to know about me. I was born into an extremely wealthy family and raised in the Bahamas."

Court didn't interrupt her. He was happy she'd decided to share part of her past.

"My parents loved to spend money," she said with a smile. "They had nice things, but they spent on others, as well. I grew up in a stunningly beautiful place with everything I could ever want. I went off to UCLA for my degree, thinking that nothing would ever change. Then my parents got into a wreck and they were both killed."

She paused and took a long drink of the beer. "Anyone's life will change with the death of their parents. But it was more. I learned that my parents were all but bankrupt, struggling to keep living as they had been and paying for my college. It was up to me to plan both of their funerals and sell everything they had to pay off the creditors."

Court hated the misery he saw on her face, but it was the glint of tears that about undid him. He could never stand to see a woman cry. It slayed him.

"All those people my parents gave to while they could were nowhere to be found. Not a single one of them helped me," Skye continued. "I had a knack for getting as much money as I could for the artwork and my mother's jewelry. That more than made up for other differences. There was nearly enough left after the bills were paid to pay for the rest of my college."

"Did you use it?"

"Some of it. I worked because I knew I had to change my life. I wouldn't always have money to fall back on. It was a lifestyle shift," she said with a grin.

The only other person who'd ever heard that story was Jo, because her college roommate had helped her find a job and learn to manage money. Skye wasn't sure why she'd shared it with Court. It left her raw, exposed.

But it also felt as if it healed her.

She watched as he hooked a finger around the longneck of the bottle and lifted it to his lips to drink. Surely he had to know how incredibly sexy he was.

It was his blond hair and the way it hit his jaw. It had more body than a man's hair had a right to. Even when he ran his fingers through it, it looked amazing.

And his eyes. Damn, the man had eyes that made her feel as if she were drowning in vivid, electric blue.

Then there was his body. With every muscle defined and sculpted to perfection, he made her mouth water.

Despite all of that, or maybe because of it, it was the way he made her feel. She felt special, as if she were the only woman on earth he cared about, and that melted her heart. He made her feel safe, secure. Something that she hadn't felt since her parents.

Skye swallowed as she realized the room had grown quiet as they stared at each other. The sexual tension was back. Truthfully, it had never left. It was only banked when he was away, but it flared to life anew when he was around.

He set his bottle down on the desk and closed the distance between them. He put a hand against the wall near her head and simply stared at her.

Skye's heart was pounding with excitement, her blood warming with need. Her gaze lowered to his mouth for a heartbeat while she struggled to keep oxygen moving through her lungs.

"Are you afraid of me?" he whispered.

"No. Never."

His hands slid to either side of her face as his lips touched hers.

Skye wanted to shout with joy. Her hands immediately rose to touch him, hating that she still held her beer in one hand. His kiss was soft, searching as he lightly kissed her a few times.

Then he groaned softly and slanted his mouth over hers. His tongue slid between her lips. She sagged against him, gripping his shirt with her free hand.

His arms shifted so that they were wrapped around her, holding her tight. The kiss deepened, and desire coiled low in her belly.

Suddenly, the beer was gone from her hand, taken by Court. He ended the kiss and lifted his head enough to look down at her.

"My God, you're beautiful."

Skye closed her eyes and rested her head on his chest as her arms wound around his neck. She had no idea how long they stood there before he set the beer down on the desk and held out his hand.

She knew what he was asking. And she knew there was never any other choice for her. She had known the first time she'd looked into his eyes that they would eventually end up at this moment.

Skye put her hand in his as she lifted her head to meet his gaze. The desire reflected in his gorgeous eyes made her catch her breath. He wanted her. And he wanted her to know it.

No one had ever looked at her so...blatantly before. It was exhilarating, thrilling. But there was another emotion reflected there. Deeper, stronger – fiercer even, an emotion that made her grip him tighter to keep standing.

The sexual tension they had been dancing around for days was no longer being ignored. It took center stage. And it was glorious.

Court's fingers slid into her hair, gently tugging

her head back. His mouth was on her exposed neck, kissing a hot trail down to her collarbone while he moved them to the bed.

CHAPTER FOURTEEN

He was in heaven. Blissful, delightful heaven.

Court couldn't stop touching her, learning her. Skye's skin was as soft as velvet. The more he touched, the more he needed. She was a drug, and after one kiss, he was addicted.

It was everything he could do to keep tight control over the need pounding through him. He wanted to toss her on the bed and cover her body with his, sliding into her until neither knew where one ended and the other began.

But Skye was different.

He wanted their time together to be different.

And God willing, it would serve as a solid foundation for something much more.

Court unbuttoned her shirt while he continued to place small kisses down to her breasts. As soon as the last button gave way, he pushed the shirt open and let his gaze feast upon her royal blue and black bra with leather trim.

It was so sexy, that for a moment, all he could do was stare at the material as his balls tightened.

"Do you like?" she asked, a grin in her voice.

Court nodded without looking up. "Please tell me you have more of these."

"I do."

"Thank goodness," he murmured.

Skye shrugged off the shirt, exposing more of her glorious skin. Court rested his hands on her ribcage and slowly caressed up and around to her back. With a twist of his fingers, he unhooked her bra. The garment sagged as the straps fell from her shoulders.

His gaze met hers then. There was no shyness, no caution. Passion shown brightly in her dark gaze. He loved a woman who knew what she wanted and wasn't embarrassed about it.

It made his own desire burn brighter, hotter. The woman had no idea how she was chipping away at his control. Court had always been able to govern his emotions.

Skye flayed him raw, leaving him bare and unprotected. He should be pushing her away, not pulling her closer. But with her, he wanted her to see all that he was – as well as all that he yearned for.

He refused to allow the walls that he usually erected between him and his lovers to come up. Skye was the kind of woman who would stand beside him, facing whatever the world decided to throw at him.

Those kinds of women were hard to come by, and Court wasn't going to let her slip through his fingers. He was going to do everything in his power to make her fall for him as he had already fallen for her.

Was it love?

If it wasn't, it was damn sure close. He might have cared for other women before, but there had never been one who brought out his protective instincts like Skye.

It wasn't just because she put herself in danger. It was the woman herself. There wasn't a part of her he wasn't completely infatuated with — including her stubbornness.

Court's hands shook when she removed the bra. He dropped his gaze back to her breasts. Unable to resist a moment longer, he cupped the globes, letting the weight of them sink into his memory.

Against his palm, her nipples hardened. The pulse at her neck was erratic, her chest rising and falling rapidly. He massaged her breasts before letting his thumbs circle her nipples until her eyes rolled back in her head.

Court smiled as he watched her. Her obvious pleasure only spiked his own. His cock ached to be free of his jeans.

He wrapped an arm around her waist as he dropped to his knees. Then he clamped his mouth around a turgid nipple and suckled it deep in his mouth.

Her answering moan was just what he needed to hear. He moved from one breast to the other. Her hands were in his hair, holding him close.

Court unbuttoned her jeans and then lowered the zipper. He slid his hands into the waist at her hips and pushed the denim down. His cock twitched as his hands traveled down one shapely leg and then the other.

When the pants were bunched at her ankles, he lifted each of her legs in turn to step out of them. With one swipe, he shoved them across the floor.

Court kissed first one hip then the other, smiling as he did when he saw the same blue with black leather trim. The woman was going to kill him with her seductive underwear.

But he loved every moment of it.

He looked up at Skye to find her watching him.

She ran her fingers through his hair. "I've dreamt of this moment. I knew it would be amazing, but I didn't realize how much."

"You've not seen anything, yet," Court said as he stood.

He was about to lift her to lay her on the bed when Skye pulled his shirt up. Court raised his arms and helped her remove it.

Somehow he stood still while her hands roamed over his chest, arms, and stomach. Everywhere she touched burned hotter, his desire increasing at a rapid rate.

Skye didn't want a single moment to pass by that she didn't remember. She touched his skin, amazed at how warm he was. He stood unmoving and let her touch every inch of his upper body. She had no idea how long she stood there before she realized his hands were fisted at his sides and his eyes were closed.

She paused, her gaze fastened to his face.

His eyes snapped open, and that's when she saw how he fought to remain immobile for her. Skye cupped his face with one hand.

Then she sat on the edge of the bed and reached for the waist of his jeans. She unfastened them and pushed them down. The jeans dropped to his ankles, and Court kicked out of them.

His arms were suddenly around her as he laid her back on the bed, kissing her as if there were no tomorrow. Skin to skin, they lay together, their bodies aflame with desire.

Skye was breathless when his mouth left hers and found her breasts again. They swelled once more, her nipples aching for his touch.

She opened her legs when he gave them a nudge with his knee. A gasp tore from her when his fingers delved into her sex and found her clit. His touch was light as he teased her swollen nub until she was panting and mindless with need.

He alternated between licking her clit and sinking his fingers deep inside her for a few thrusts. Skye was on the precipice of an orgasm for the longest time. Then it hit her.

Court watched her back arch, her mouth open on a silent scream as her body jerked with her climax. It was the most beautiful thing he had ever seen. And he wanted to see it every day for the rest of his life.

He rose over her, his cock at her entrance. She was so wet he slid in easily. Her eyes opened to look at him as he pushed deeper.

With his teeth clenched, he thrust deeper into her tight sheath that fit him like a glove. He moved slowly, savoring every minute until he was fully seated within, an overwhelming sense of completeness washing over him.

Then he rolled onto his back, taking Skye with him. She smiled as she straddled him and sat up. A second later, she was rocking her hips.

Court hissed in a breath at the amazing feelings rushing through him. There was a slight clatter hitting the windows and he realized it was raining.

Skye moved faster and faster, pulling Court with her. He rolled her nipples between his fingers as she rode him. It wasn't long before she leaned down, her long curtain of black hair surrounding him.

He gazed into her dark eyes. As they made love, the attraction was strengthening into something much stronger. He could see it reflected in her eyes, and he knew she saw it in his.

Court pulled her down for a kiss and rolled her once more onto her back. Then he rose up on his hands and began to thrust hard and fast.

She gasped and ended the kiss as she clawed the comforter. Her legs wrapped around his waist, urging him faster. He didn't look away from her as he took them both higher and higher.

He wasn't ready for it to end when the orgasm claimed Skye once more. The feel of her body clamping around him was too much. He thrust twice more before his climax swept through him.

Emotion, deep and uncharted, filled Court when Skye wrapped her arms around him and simply held on. They lay with their limbs tangled, listening to the rain.

The night had changed him. Suddenly, he understood why Solomon kept his distance from women, because Court wasn't sure if he could survive losing Skye now.

She was part of his soul, part of his essence.

Part of his heart.

He knew without a doubt that it was love. He had fallen in love and hadn't even known it until that moment. Love had a way of sneaking up on people that way. It couldn't have come at a worse time, but it only spurred Court to think of other ways he could keep Skye safe.

Because he would walk through Hell itself if that's what it took.

Court stared out the window from the bed, watching the water run down the glass. He felt as tall as a giant with the love inside him. But he also felt as helpless as a newborn. It was a frightening situation he found himself in. Not that he would change a minute of it.

"The first thing we need to do when we leave this house is go find you more of that sexy underwear," Court said, hoping to lighten his own mood.

Skye chuckled. "I had no idea you would like it so much."

"I should've paid more attention when I opened that drawer of yours and tossed everything in a bag. I may have to go back."

She didn't laugh again as he had hoped. Instead, she let out a deep breath. "I'm really scared."

He lifted his head from her chest to look at her. "Don't be. I won't let anyone get you."

"Things happen." She smiled sadly, her dark eyes holding a frown. "Accidents happen."

"Not to you. Not with me."

She laid her palm on the side of his face. "I don't want to freak you out, and I probably shouldn't say this, but I care deeply about you."

"I feel the same." It was on the tip of his tongue to tell her he loved her, but not yet. The time would come soon.

"I'm glad," she said with a nod, dropping her hand. "I don't know what's going to happen tomorrow, but no matter what, I want you to know this night has meant the world to me."

Nothing was going to happen to her. Court refused to let her get hurt. She was his love, the woman he never expected to find.

"I read your article," he said.

Her eyes widened. "Really? I kept waiting for someone to say something."

"I knew you would send it in. It was good."

She glanced down. "I was trying to fix what I did. Not sure I succeeded."

"It's a start." He was proud that she had taken a

step back from telling the world where the supernatural lived and what they looked like, to helping people understand the dangers of the unexplained around them. "What did Helen think about it?"

"She changed some of it to make it scarier," Skye said with a frown. "She wanted me to rewrite it, but I refused. I'm surprised she even ran the article."

Court propped his head up on an elbow. "You're talented. You'll find another job if you need to."

"I'm talented, huh?" she asked with a smile.

"Extremely."

Her smile faded as she became serious once more. "I hate that I wrote the article that got me in this mess, but it brought you to my door. That I'm most thankful for."

"Not nearly as much as me. Whether you know it or not, Skye Parrish, you've changed me."

He took her mouth in another kiss as thunder rumbled around them, desire taking them once more.

CHAPTER FIFTEEN

Skye woke to the sound of rain. She was lying on Court's chest, his arm wrapped around her. She opened her eyes and shifted her head to look at him. A smile formed when she saw his other arm propped behind his head as he watched her.

"Was I snoring?" she asked.

He winked. "A little."

Skye laughed as she ducked her head. "Great."

"It was a cute little half-snore."

"There's no such thing."

"There is now."

He kissed the top of her head, and Skye didn't think a day could start any better. His arm tightened, drawing her closer.

"How did you sleep?" he asked.

"Like the dead. How about you?"

"Good."

She shifted to prop her head up on her hand to see him. "Liar. Did you sleep at all?"

"I dozed," he admitted. "It was nice to hold you. Even nicer to wake up with you."

Skye was going to die of pleasure. Court's words weren't false charm. She could see he meant them. "Can we stop time for a few hours?"

"If only I could," he said and fingered a lock of her hair.

She fell onto her back and looked at the ceiling. "It'll work. Minka's idea is solid."

"And puts you in danger again."

"There's no way around that," Skye said as she turned her head to him. "They want me."

Court sat up and leaned against the headboard. "I got you first."

His jest made her smile again. "Keep talking like that and I won't ever leave this room."

"Now you're speaking my language," he said as he leaned over her with a sexy half-smile.

She could feel his arousal against her leg. Skye reached down and wrapped her hand around him, slowly moving her hand up and down his length.

He moaned low in his throat, his eyes closing. It didn't matter how many times they had made love through the night, Skye wanted him again. He knew where to kiss, how to touch to send her spiraling.

Her body yearned for his touch, for him to fill her again. She loved his weight atop her. More than that, she loved him inside her, his rod sliding in and out, thrusting deep enough to touch her womb.

Skye never knew she was such a wanton. Then again, Court brought out many things in her she hadn't known. It was because he was with her that she had slept so soundly.

Suddenly, she found herself flipped onto her stomach. Court's large hands grabbed her hips and lifted her butt up into the air. Her hands fisted the covers as his fingers delved into her sex to make sure she was wet.

And then the blunt head of his arousal entered her. Skye closed her eyes in pleasure as he filled her, stretching her. Her body was pleasantly sore, but that didn't stop her from wanting more.

She rose up on her hands and looked over her shoulder at him. His chest rumbled with another groan as he leaned over her. One hand remained on her hips as he thrust while the other cupped her breast and tweaked her nipple.

Skye moaned and rocked her hips back against him. Her body was primed, ready for another orgasm, and when his fingers found her clit, she instantly climaxed.

The force of it took her breath away. He held her until her body stopped shaking. Then he held her hips and began to thrust. He went deeper, harder. Faster.

He held her so she couldn't move, so that she clamped down on him every time he entered her. Soon she felt him shudder as he orgasmed.

They fell to the side, laughing as the rain hit the window harder. Court nuzzled the back of her neck while her sated body relaxed against him.

"Should we go down soon?" she asked.

Court shook his head. "They won't bother us, or think twice about us being up here the rest of the day."

"But your brothers will need you."

He sighed. "Probably."

"I also know how you want to be in the middle of the planning."

Court kissed her ear. "You know me well."

She was beginning to, but she knew there was much more of him to learn. And she couldn't wait to start.

"Why don't you get in the shower," he suggested.

Skye scooted out of his arms to the side of the bed. She looked back at him and smiled before disappearing into the bathroom.

Court waited until the door closed behind her before he fell back and put his hand over his arm. He had run through Minka's plan over in his head all night. It was a solid plan. But there were still things that could go wrong. Every time he thought of one of them, his heart felt as if it were encased in ice.

He rose and wrapped a blanket around his waist as he walked from the room down the hall to Solomon's room. He didn't stop until he reached the master bath and shut the door. Then he took a quick shower, not bothering to shave.

In less than ten minutes, he was out and dressed in fresh clothes. He paused beside his room and listened to the shower running. Quietly, he walked inside and got his boots. Then he walked back out and down the stairs.

He was putting on his shoes on the bottom step when Kane walked from the back of the house into the foyer. Court nodded to his brother.

"I'm glad you took my advice," Kane said. "You look better."

Court finished with his boots and stood. He punched Kane in the shoulder with a grin. "Mind your own business."

A small smile began to form but didn't reach its full potential. "Minka's plan is in action. Griffin and a few of his men spread the rumor through the Quarter last night."

"There's no going back now," Court said, glancing back at his room.

Kane grunted. "This needs to be taken care of now."

"I know."

"Nothing will happen to her," Kane stated.

Court ran a hand through his still-wet hair. "Yeah."

He and Kane walked to the kitchen where Myles, Addison, and Riley were. Myles was stuffing the last of his breakfast in his mouth when they walked in. He kissed Addison and waved at them as he hurried out the back door.

"Morning," Riley said.

Court pulled out a chair and sat at the table. "Morning. Smells good, cuz."

Riley flashed him a bright smile. "That's

because my cooking is awesome. I'm nearly as good as Beau."

Everyone knew that her brother was one of the best cooks around, hands down. Court watched Addison look worriedly out the back door.

A moment later, Solomon opened the door and walked in. He stopped at the entry and shook water from his hair and clothes. Riley threw him a towel, and he wiped as much off as he could.

As soon as he spotted Court, he walked to the table and took the chair opposite him at the rectangular table. "Did Kane fill you in?"

"He did," Court said. "How do you feel about it?"

"We're all ready." Solomon stared at him intently. "And you? How do you feel?"

Like he was about to puke. "Good."

"I keep telling him he's not a good liar," Skye said from behind him.

Court turned and instantly held out his hand to her. Her lips turned upward in a grin as she came to him, their fingers sliding together. Court pulled out the chair next to him with his foot and she sat.

"He's worried," Kane said.

Skye lifted one shoulder in a shrug. "So am I. But it has to be done. None of us can continue like this."

"We could call in our cousins," Solomon offered.

Court looked at Riley to see her shoulders stiffen. Then she turned to them. "If we need them, then do it. Now."

"And give Delphine another go at them?" Court asked. "I don't think so. We've got the Moonstone clan helping. That should be enough."

Solomon ran a hand down his face, the weariness showing. "It better be. We're putting a lot of faith in the witch."

"Minka knows what she's doing," Addison said.

Kane nodded. "I agree. It'll work."

Court wasn't willing to bet Skye's life on it. Then again, if he didn't, her life was still in jeopardy. It was a no-win situation, and it sucked. Royally.

"Y'all didn't have to get up so early," Riley said with a wink to Court and Skye.

Skye laughed. "We were hungry."

"All you had to was shout from the room," Addison said with a big smile. "We would've brought some food up."

Court looked around the kitchen. This was his family. It kept growing, and he was glad of it. It added more worry, but the more of them that joined together, the stronger they were.

He wondered if Kane would ever get past what had happened and be happy again. Until he could, he would never make room in his life for a woman.

Then there was Solomon. His eldest brother was beyond frustrating most days. Yet, Court held out hope with Minka. The way the two of them rubbed each other raw could be because they both fought their desires.

Or it could mean they really hated each other.

Minka walked in at that moment. Solomon

didn't even look at her as he poured himself some coffee. Minka smiled at everyone, but she also refrained from looking Solomon's way.

The back door opened and Griffin came inside. His attention was instantly on Minka.

"I could hear you, you know," she said to Solomon. "If you don't like my plan, then come up with another one."

Solomon kept his face averted. His lips peeled back in a sneer. "Do you think we weren't trying to come up with something?"

"With you, I don't know," Minka replied sarcastically.

Griffin smiled at Minka. "Solomon might not like your idea, but I think it's a good one. Anything else you need help with?"

"No, thank you," Minka said sweetly.

Court slid his gaze to Solomon to see a muscle twitch in his jaw. Riley put the bacon and eggs on the table, along with sausage and biscuits. Everyone had a seat except for Minka, who was pouring herself some coffee.

She turned around and saw the only open chair was next to Solomon, putting her between him and Griffin. Court shared a secret look with Skye, who also noticed the situation.

Skye leaned over. "Do you think she knows Griffin is into her?"

"Definitely," Court whispered.

Skye then asked in a low voice, "Does Solomon really not like her?"

Court moved aside her hair so his lips were by

her ear. "I think the point is that he likes her. A lot."

"I don't understand," she said as she leaned back, frowning.

"His fiancée was killed years ago," Court whispered.

Skye's mouth formed a big O. Enough years had passed that Solomon could talk freely about it, but Court wasn't going to bring it up unless Solomon did.

There was small chitchat around the table as they ate. Despite the group, Court felt as if it were just him and Skye. He couldn't look at her without smiling, his love growing by the second.

"Ugh," Riley said with a roll of her eyes. "I can't sit at this table a minute longer and see the two of y'all making eyes at each other. The smiles and secret looks are driving me batty." She rose and looked pointedly at Court. "You do realize I'm single, right? Geesh. You two are worse than Addison and Myles."

"Amen," Kane said as he rose and gathered some dishes to bring to the sink.

Addison merely smiled. "I think it's cute."

Court's smile died when his gaze went to Solomon. Because he knew his brother was remembering Misty.

And how he had lost her.

Suddenly, the food in Court's stomach turned sour. It was going to be a long damn day.

CHAPTER SIXTEEN

Skye didn't think she had ever been so nervous in her entire life. Her hands shook, her palms were sweating, and at any moment, she expected to lose what little bit of food was in her stomach.

She leaned against the porch column watching as Court and his brothers left. The Moonstone pack had already made themselves scarce hours before. Now it was just Skye, Addison, Riley, and Minka in the house.

A house, which hours before had felt so comforting and safe, seemed ominous and...empty.

Skye put on a brave face for Court, even though she was trembling inside. He hadn't wanted to leave. In fact, it had taken all of them – especially her – to convince him that it would all work out.

Right before he stepped off the porch, he had

pulled her against him, nuzzling her neck. Then he had whispered, "I won't be far. I'll be near, ready to kill any vamp who comes for you."

He kissed her, hard. But it was full of passion and promise. Then he whispered something beneath his breath that had made Skye's heart skip a beat.

She wasn't completely certain, but it had sounded very much like 'I love you.'

Skye bit her tongue so she wouldn't call out to Court and beg him to remain. She touched her lips, her eyes filling with tears. She loved him. Desperately.

"I love you, Court LaRue," she whispered, hoping the wind carried her words to him.

When she could no longer see Court after he'd faded into the woods, Skye turned around and saw Minka standing at the screen door.

Minka blinked and looked at her as she pushed open the door. "We have a little over an hour until dusk."

"Right," Addison said and turned away from the porch railing to walk into the house.

Riley was next, a frown marring her forehead.

Skye grabbed the screen door. "What is there to do other than wait?"

"Lots," Minka said with a smile. "This house is protected, but I've been adding to them for the past few days."

Skye stepped into the house and let the screen door close behind her. Then she shut the door. "Court said for us not to leave the house, so we should be fine."

"Oh, girl," Minka said as she linked her arm with Skye's. "You know the supernatural, but you don't really know them."

"What's that mean?"

"It means that they'll get you out of the house any way they can."

Skye tried to swallow, but her mouth was too dry. She had been pretty confident that Minka's idea would work. Now she was beginning to understand Solomon's reluctance, and Court's nervousness.

"The boys won't be far," Minka hurried to say. "Court won't let anything happen. He cares deeply for you."

"And I for him. That does neither of us any good right now."

"You'd be surprised," Riley said from the doorway of the kitchen. She smiled and waved them toward her. "Love has a way of beating the odds sometimes."

Skye thought of her parents. "And others?"

"My parents were murdered by a vengeful woman who wanted my father for herself," Riley said. She shrugged as if it happened every day.

But Skye saw the pain in her gaze.

Addison was leaning against the kitchen counters. "Solomon's fiancée was killed right in front of his eyes. He couldn't reach her in time."

"I had no idea," Minka replied softly.

Skye walked to the fridge for a beer, but as she looked at the bottles, she knew she needed something stronger. She closed the refrigerator door and asked, "Where is the alcohol?"

It was Riley who walked out of the room and returned a few minutes later with a bottle of vodka and a bottle of bourbon. She held each up. Addison chose the vodka while Skye picked the bourbon.

"What happened to Solomon's woman?" Minka asked.

Riley poured herself some bourbon and sat at the table. "The specifics are never discussed. I know she was killed, and that Solomon blames himself."

"How long ago?" Skye asked.

Addison tossed back a shot of vodka. "Several years. It's why you never see him with anyone."

"He refuses to let another woman close," Riley said.

Skye sipped her bourbon. "I can understand that after such a tragedy."

"We're not going to end up like her," Addison said. She set down the glass and looked at each of them. "We know what's coming. We know what they want. And we have a witch on our side."

Minka's smile was slight. "I'm here to help in any way I can, but until we know who it is that's helping the vampires, we can only wait."

"Personally, I think you're damn brilliant," Riley said to Minka.

The witch shrugged, though she beamed from the praise. "I wanted to help."

"Still," Skye said, impressed herself. "I would

never have thought to spread a rumor to have them show up."

Addison smiled. "I know, right? Most want to keep hidden. But not Minka. She puts it all out there."

"We were in the middle of it not that long ago," Minka said to Addison. "Running doesn't do any good."

Skye knew the truth of that. The past week had been both tiring and wonderful. Yet it was no way to live. For any of them. She owed each person there a debt she would most likely never be able to repay, but she was going to try.

"It feels weird not having the guys in the house," Skye said.

Riley's lips twisted. "I have to agree that I miss seeing those sexy Moonstone wolves. Especially Griffin. Can we say yum?"

"I've seen how some of them look at you," Addison said to Riley. "You won't be single long with that bunch."

"Now that's what I'm talking about." Riley held up her glass and tossed back the contents. "It's been awhile since I've been kissed. Between Addison and Myles and now Court and Skye, I'm feeling the need for a man."

Addison was still smiling when she turned her gaze to Minka. "I'm pretty sure if Minka gave Griffin even a hint that she was interested, she would have some company, as well."

Minka rolled her eyes. "I've got enough to occupy my time, thank you very much. A man just complicates things."

"Unless he's worth it," Skye added, thinking of Court.

Who was more than worth it.

"Can't argue with that," Riley said.

Minka cleared her throat. "Let's get down to business, girls. The house is warded, but none of you are. I'm going to change that. I've made these," she said and set three bracelets on the table.

Skye sat forward to peer at them closer. The bracelets were silver, each a different design. Minka handed Addison a bracelet with long links. Riley was given one with several small cords of silver that were braided.

Minka then handed the last bracelet to Skye. Skye accepted the piece of jewelry, running her fingers along the two bands of silver. They looked dainty, but they were hard and substantial. Anchoring the two bands on either side was an oval with a fleur de lis etched in it.

Skye slipped the bracelet on her wrist. The bangle felt right resting against her skin. She looked up at Minka and smiled.

"Will this keep the vampires away from us?" Riley asked.

Minka shoved her long curls over her shoulder. "Hopefully it'll keep everything away from you. Including Delphine," she said, looking pointedly at Riley.

Skye frowned. That name again. She was truly an enemy of both the Chiassons and the LaRues. And she sounded awful.

"She knows you're here," Minka continued. "She's already tried to kill your brothers. It's only a matter of time before she turns to you."

Riley put her bracelet in place and smiled. "Let the bitch try."

"The bracelets will stop some magic, but not all of it. No ward will stop all magic. If whoever is after you is smart enough and has enough time, they can figure a way to get to you."

"We'll keep that in mind," Skye said. She touched the bracelet with her left hand. "If I do leave the house, will the bracelet keep the vampires away from me?"

Minka nodded. "It should. Keep in mind we still don't know who is working with the vamps. I used wards that will protect y'all against anyone – human or supernatural – out to harm you. It covers a broad range but could leave a gap open where the bracelets won't work."

"Where is yours?" Addison asked.

Minka linked her fingers together on the table. "I have my own wards."

Skye glanced out the window. The sun was sinking rapidly. It wouldn't be too much longer before the vampires surrounded the LaRue house.

Who else would be with them? The Djinn? The witches? Delphine?

"You aren't in this alone," Riley said as she laid a hand on Skye's arm.

Skye swiveled her head to the pretty brunette. "I know, and I can't tell you how thankful I am for that. I don't think I could do this alone."

"Yes you could." Addison smiled when Skye shot her a surprised look. "We're all stronger than we think we are. You proved that already, Skye."

Skye choked on a laugh. "By running?"

"By standing against the vampires with a knife," Minka said.

"I only had the courage to do it because I knew Court was there and the rest of you were outside the club."

Riley snorted loudly. "Whatever the reason, you impressed the hell out of me. I hate vampires."

"Ditto," Addison said with a shiver. "I had my own run-in with one."

Skye was intrigued now. "What happened?"

Addison smiled widely. "Myles ripped his throat out with his teeth."

They all laughed. Though Skye's mind turned to Court and how he had shifted to a wolf at the vampire club. His teeth had been scary sharp, not to mention long. And he snapped his jaws with a force that meant anything in his way was going to be cut in half.

Court's family had suffered their own tragedies. It was a wonder they could continue on as they did, but it was because they had a mission to carry out.

"For the first time in a long time I have something to live for," Skye said. She tucked her hair behind her ear. "I've been wandering for so long, angry at the supernatural around me. Yet it brought me to this city and put me in Court's path. I...I don't want to lose him."

Riley sat back in her chair with a grin. "Trust

me, Court isn't going to let you go anywhere. He's a wolf, an alpha, and once they find their women, they don't let go."

"I can attest to that," Addison said with a wink.

"I love him." Skye laughed after she let the words pass her lips. "I do. I love him."

Minka's smile was a little sad. "I think we all figured that out already."

"We'll get through this night because we stand together, Skye," Riley said. "The LaRues have always been good for this city. They're good men, but more than that, they're feared and respected here."

"That's right," Minka added. "Unfortunately, that means that if the LaRues show an ounce of weakness, the rest of the factions will see it."

Skye took a deep breath. She looked from Addison to Riley, and then focused on Minka. The witch was the only one who didn't have a tie to the LaRues. "No matter what happens to me, don't let them show any weakness. Remind them what they stand for and what their presence means to the city."

"I will," Minka pledged.

Skye looked out the window to see the last rays of the sun disappear. The time had arrived.

CHAPTER SEVENTEEN

Court was restless, edgy. He didn't like leaving Skye behind. Despite him knowing it was the only way to end this thing the vampires had out for her once and for all.

The minutes ticked by as slow as centuries. He thought the sun would never set. Then as soon as it did, he wished it hadn't.

Myles and Kane had already shifted. They were on patrol on the back side of the house. Court flexed his hand as he felt his wolf urging him to give in and shift. But he waited. He was faster, stronger...deadlier in wolf form. Yet he felt the need to fight as a man, not a werewolf.

In the end, his wolf would win. Until then, he was in control.

"You're smarter than I was," Solomon

whispered.

Court frowned and jerked his head to his brother. "What?"

"With your woman. I didn't think anything could touch mine." Solomon's smile was full of regret and guilt. "I assumed that the other factions would leave us alone."

Court had never heard Solomon talk of Misty or himself this way. It took him aback to the point that he didn't know what to say.

"You've always been cautious," Court said.

Solomon shook his head. "Not always. I learned my lesson the hard way. The same won't happen to you."

"Because we planned this out?"

"Because you're not as prideful as I was." Solomon looked at the ground. "All hell is liable to break loose this night. It doesn't matter who is working with the vampires because all the factions will be watching us."

Court understood what Solomon was saying. "We can't show any weakness."

"Not even a drop. If we lose our foothold of authority, we'll be descended upon by all the factions within days."

Their hold had always been precarious no matter what generation it was. It wasn't easy being a LaRue, but it was a position Court relished.

"I have your back, little brother," Solomon said.

Court watched Solomon shift into a wolf, his clothes shredding and falling to the ground before Solomon trotted off. A moment later, Court gave into the wolf within him and shifted, as well.

He took in a deep breath. Even a mile away from the house he could smell Skye. Her scent was distinctive, alluring. She meant everything to him. He hadn't had the balls to tell her when he'd left, but he wished he had. His whispered words were for him.

His gaze lifted to the sky. The moon was climbing fast. By now his brothers would've taken their positions around the house. The Moonstone clan were behind them. Griffin's weres were always ready to fight, especially against vampires or Delphine.

Court never thought to see the Moonstone pack return to New Orleans, but he was immensely glad Griffin had brought them back to the city where they belonged. The werewolves were no longer a minority within the factions. Their numbers were increasing daily.

But right now, Court's attention was on the vampires after his woman. He crouched behind a clump of young pines and waited, hidden by their branches. His hiding spot was along the most direct route to the house from the city, but none of them expected his to be the only one used.

None of the weres were to attack any faction until the vampires attacked the house. Hopefully, they would also learn who was working with the bloodsuckers.

Court's paw dug into the ground, muddy from the recent rain. His ears turned backward as he heard movement. It was faint, almost as if it never was. But he wasn't fooled. The supernatural were gifted in all ways.

Then again, so was he.

The first vampire walked by him so close that he could have leaned over and snapped his teeth around his ankle. Instead, Court let him go.

"You don't really believe the LaRues left, do you?" a female vamp asked the man next to her as they walked toward the house.

The male chuckled softly. "I do. Stupid werewolves think they will find us all at the club to teach us a lesson. We'll be the ones to teach them."

Court's lip lifted in a snarl, but he held his growl back before any sound could be made. Fury sped through him. He might have been too young to get revenge for his parents' murder, but he was strong enough now to ensure his woman was well protected.

It took everything he had to let those vampires walk away. More and more vamps were coming, spreading out through the forest. Most didn't even look around for enemies. They had truly bought the rumor Markus had begun the day before that the LaRues were coming for the vampires at the Viper's Nest.

The sheer number of vampires worried Court. He was more than up for a fight, but his concern was for Skye. She feared the vamps. After what had happened to her both in California and in New Orleans, she had every right.

It tore at Court that he wasn't at her side to help her. His only consolation was the fact that

Riley, Minka, and Addison were with Skye. Riley was more than proficient in hunting and killing the supernatural.

And Minka...well, the witch had skills. She'd saved Myles from certain death when he'd had silver in his system.

Addison wasn't a shrinking violet. She had been learning from both Myles and Riley how to fight and hunt. Soon, she would be more than capable of taking care of herself.

After Court saw Skye in the vampire club slashing at the vampires, he knew she wouldn't curl up in a ball and wait for death to find her. It still didn't make it any easier for him.

Another five minutes passed before Court could take it no longer. He leapt from his hiding spot and clamped his teeth around the neck of a vampire. They fell to the ground as Court twisted his head, snapping the vamp's neck and ripping out his throat at the same time.

He saw movement behind him as the Moonstone weres began to silently take out any vampire near them. Court turned back toward the house and saw a vampire watching them.

Court started running, the ground blurring beneath him. He had to reach the vampire before it alerted the others that it was a trap. Court leapt and landed on the vampire just as he shouted. His voice gurgled as Court removed his throat.

But it was too late. The damage had already been done.

All around him vampires turned in his

direction, hissing their fury. He growled, hunkering down and showing his fangs. They wanted a fight. And they were going to get one.

~ ~ ~

Skye jerked when the first thud hit the house. All four of them jumped up from the table and rushed to the front of the house.

"Well shit," Riley mumbled as she looked out the window.

Addison paled as she turned to Skye. "There are so many of them."

Minka ran to the back and returned a few minutes later. "They're surrounding the house."

Skye began to panic. Then she saw the bracelet and remembered that both she and the house were warded. It was going to be all right. It had to be.

"We only want Skye," came a male voice from outside. "Send her out, and the rest of you will be unharmed."

Riley motioned for them to hide. Then she opened the front door and glared at the vampires through the screen door. She crossed her arms over her chest. "Do everyone a favor and go away. You're not getting near Skye."

"You're alone, woman," the vampire said.

Riley snorted. "Do you honestly think I need a man to protect me?"

"You're not supernatural."

"Nope. That I'm not. What I am is a Chiasson."

Skye leaned to the side of the doorway and saw

the vampires muttering among themselves. If Riley has been keeping who she was a secret, she'd just told the entire city.

Skye couldn't see much of the male, all she could tell was that he was tall. She wished she could see his face for future reference. It galled her that they all knew who she was, but she didn't know them.

"We only want Skye," the male vampire said again.

Riley dropped her arms. "Get it through your thick skull, vamp. You're not coming near her."

The vampire stepped away from the others. "You think you're untouchable because the house is warded? Think again, human."

"Please, try something. I've not been hunting in a week, and I'd like nothing better than to take your head."

Skye covered her mouth with her hand as she hid her laughter at Riley's arrogance. The smile vanished when a vampire rushed the house. As soon as he reached the porch, he was thrown backward.

Again and again the vampires charged the house. Riley calmly closed the door then stalked to the coat closet and pulled out a crossbow.

"Well, that certainly worked," Minka said as she walked into the foyer.

Riley rolled her eyes. "It was better than letting them think we were huddled in here scared."

"Everyone get a weapon," Addison said.

Riley rested the crossbow on her shoulder.

"Done."

Minka held up her hands and wiggled her fingers. "I am the weapon."

"True," Addison said with a smile. She then began to load a revolver with silver bullets. "Skye?"

Skye touched her waist where the silver-bladed knife rested in its scabbard. "Got it. How long can the wards hold up?"

"Forever with idiots like these," Minka said.

No sooner had the words left her mouth than the house shook as if the ground had shifted beneath them. Skye reached out her arms, grabbing anything she could to keep standing. She jerked her gaze to Minka to find the witch's face lined with worry.

"That was bad," Riley said.

Minka nodded. "Very."

Addison grabbed the box of silver bullets. "How long do we have until they're past the wards?"

"Seconds."

Skye's ears rang from the loud boom around them so she didn't know who'd said it, but it didn't matter. The vampires were breaking through the wards.

"We need to get outside," Minka shouted.

Skye shook her head. "Court said to remain here."

Minka rushed to her. "Look, if we stay inside, they'll break through the wards. The wards need to remain intact so that we have a place to come to."

"But won't they know how to break them

later?"

Minka shook her head. "They're throwing every bit of magic they have at it."

"Who is?"

"The Djinn."

Skye's legs buckled. She grabbed the banister to keep her feet. "That's who teamed up with the vamps?"

"Looks that way," Riley said, her hand on the doorknob. "Everyone ready?"

Skye walked to the door. "Not in the least."

"Me either," Riley said with a wink.

Then Riley threw open the door.

CHAPTER EIGHTEEN

He was so busy killing vampires that it took Court a moment to realize he wasn't the only one. He stood with his front paws on the chest of a dead vamp on the ground as his gaze fastened on none other than Scott.

His one-time friend had some gall being there taking advantage of the situation by killing supernatural beings. Scott was dead wrong if he thought he would be able to sneak up on Court and kill him.

Scott swung his axe, beheading the vampire he was fighting. His chest heaved and sweat ran down his face. The black tee he wore was splattered with blood, as were his arms, neck, and face.

He turned his head and looked at Court. His lips parted as if he were going to talk. Just then,

Court spied a vampire stalking Scott. Court took off running, tackling the vampire and killing him quickly.

If anyone was going to kill Scott, it was going to be Court. He swiveled his head and growled at Scott.

"I know you don't want me here," Scott said. "But I wasn't going to sit by and not help."

Court turned away from him. He didn't want to hear anything Scott had to say because nothing could make up for the betrayal.

A howl sliced through the air. Court stilled, his heart thumping hard against his ribs. He recognized the howl as Kane's, alerting him that the women were out of the house.

Court looked around at the dead vampires littering the ground. There were many of them, but not nearly enough. It was time to close in on the trap.

He started toward the house when Scott stepped in front of him. Court bared his teeth and growled.

"Let me help," Scott said.

Court lunged and snapped his jaws.

A frown marred Scott's face. "What is with you? You're not the type to decline such an offer in this situation."

Court didn't have time for this. He rushed past Scott, his mind on Skye. For every vamp he closed in on as he ate up the ground, he killed them. Then he reached the edge of the trees and saw the vampires surrounding the house. But that was nothing compared to seeing Skye standing in front of the house. It made his heart stop.

She was supposed to remain inside. If she and the others hadn't, it was for good reason. Out of the corner of his eye, he saw movement.

The Moonstone pack was slowly closing in on the vampires. They were all crouched low to the ground, their gazes trained on the enemy.

Court was about to take out a vampire when he caught sight of a Djinn. So that's who was helping the vampires.

To Court's left was Gage, Griffin's brother. He saw the Djinn, as well. The Djinn normally kept to themselves, distrusting everyone. It would have to take something big to have them partner with the vampires, which meant it had to be more than Skye's article.

The Djinn's magic was fierce. They were never easy to take down, but the LaRues had had run-ins with them before. Court wasn't afraid to fight them. He was afraid of Skye being harmed in the process.

With a nod to Gage, Court leapt in the middle of the vampires and began sinking his teeth into them.

~ ~ ~

Skye was so afraid, that for a moment she couldn't move. The vampire numbers were impressive, but it was the Djinn standing in front of them that stole her breath.

"Silver works on the Djinn, as well," Riley said to her.

Skye pulled out her knife, wishing it were a bit longer. Something like a machete. Or a sword. A sword would be awesome in this instance. Really, anything that would keep the monsters from getting close.

Everyone stood staring at each other, the silence deafening. Not even the animals of the bayou dared to make a sound. It was as if the world held its breath waiting to see what would happen.

Suddenly, Skye saw a blur of tawny fur in the moonlight in front of her. Court. He attacked the vampires, and immediately after that, there were werewolves everywhere.

Some vampires tried to scatter to get away, but there were more weres waiting for them in the trees. Other vampires took the opportunity to try and kill the weres. They succeeded in taking out six werewolves, too.

The male vampire who'd spoken earlier, those closest to him, as well as the Djinn focused on Skye, Riley, Addison, and Minka.

Riley fired the crossbow, landing an arrow in the forehead of a Djinn. Those around him paused and watched as he fell back, dead.

Riley smiled and quickly loaded another silver-tipped arrow. "Come on, you ugly douches. It's time to die."

That's all it took for the vampires and Djinn to rush them. Skye could do nothing more than keep slashing her blade, praying that neither of them could touch her. Because if they did, they could put her under the same spell as before.

~ ~ ~

Court finished off another kill and felt the slash of a vampire's nails in his fur. Blood ran down his flank as he whirled around, snapping his jaws.

Before he could attack, Gage locked his jaws around the vamp's throat. Court let Gage finish him off as he turned to look for Skye.

He saw the vampire leaders, including Jacques and Anton, surrounding her. The Djinn in the mix only made things more dangerous. Court spotted Skye doing her best to hold her own with Minka on one side of her and Riley on the other.

Minka was doing a fine job with her magic keeping the Djinn at bay, but the Djinn were quickly weakening her. Court attacked the Djinn closest to him. His jaws clamped on his arm, halting him long enough for Skye to plunge her dagger into his heart.

Between the vampires' claws and the Djinn's magic, there wasn't an inch on Court that didn't have a wound. A Djinn rushed Riley, knocking her to the ground so that the crossbow flew from her hands.

A second later, Gage was on the Djinn. Riley rolled over to get an arrow. She sat up and thrust it in the side of the Djinn's head.

Court stayed close to Skye. When he next looked up, Kane, Solomon, Myles, and Griffin were there, as well. Court felt as if the tide were turning in their favor. Right up until a Djinn got too close to Skye while Court was fighting a vampire.

The Djinn touched her, and Skye screamed and flew backward to lay unmoving. Court rushed to her, standing over her with his teeth bared. His gaze was locked on the Djinn who had hurt his woman. The savage would die. Painfully.

Court ducked a flare of magic from the Djinn, but he wasn't quick enough. It slammed into him, the pain causing his limbs to freeze. When he was able to open his eyes, he was no longer a wolf.

He glanced at Skye and saw her knife inches from her hand. Court acted as if he was too weak to sit up and fell sideways. As soon as his hand closed around the hilt of the weapon, he slowly climbed to his feet.

"Are you ready to die?" the Djinn asked, his black tattoos covering his bald head so thickly that there was barely an inch of skin not marked.

Court pushed back the pain from his many injuries. "Are you?"

"I'm not the one weakened to such a state," the Djinn stated. His gaze was contemptuous as he looked Court up and down. "Look at you. A LaRue werewolf taken to protecting a human who would expose us."

"She's my woman."

The Djinn's smile was slow and evil. "In that case, I'll make sure she suffers even more. Perhaps I won't kill you. I'll take you with us and make you watch what I do to her."

"Do you really think you can?"

"The LaRues are no longer as strong as they once were. Your time in the Quarter is finished."

Court tightened his grip on the knife. "Then come and get me."

The noise of the battle faded as Court focused on the Djinn. He knew exactly what the Djinn would do to Skye, and it was worse than the vampires turning her.

But that wasn't going to happen.

Court waited for the Djinn to get closer. He swung the dagger up into the Djinn's mouth through his chin the same instant a shot rang out and slammed into the Djinn's head.

He pulled the blade from the Djinn and turned to Skye. He gathered her in his arms and held her while gently stroking her face.

"It's over," Riley said as she came to stand beside him. "The remaining vampires and Djinn are leaving."

Court looked up to find his brothers surrounding him still in wolf form. The Moonstone wolves slowly made their way to them.

"Thank you all," Court said to everyone. "We couldn't have done this without you. The werewolves have been absent from New Orleans for too long. This is your home. Our home. We showed the factions that tonight."

Minka squatted down beside him and touched Skye's head. "She was given a heavy dose of magic, but she'll wake up soon."

"Thank you," Court told her.

Minka smiled. "It's my pleasure."

"The others know you're not dead now."

She shrugged. "It was bound to happen eventually. I'll deal with it."

"We'll deal with it," he corrected her. "You're not alone in this."

Minka stood and moved away, but Court noticed that Solomon walked so that he was near her. Court gathered Skye in his arms and got to his feet. Addison, Riley, and Minka were careful to keep their gazes away from him since he was nude.

He was about to turn to go into the house when Kane issued a growl. Court watched as Scott rolled a vampire off him and got on his hands and knees before he stood. Scott looked around until he saw Court.

That's when Court saw the gun in Scott's hand. So that's who had shot the Djinn he'd been fighting. He should thank Scott for that, but then again, none of them would be here if Scott hadn't betrayed him.

"You should leave," Court told Scott. "You're not welcome here."

Scott holstered his gun and ran a hand through his hair. "All because I couldn't handle my best friend being a werewolf?"

Kane growled again, Myles joining in when Scott tried to walk near. Scott stopped, his hands up.

Court shook his head. "You betrayed us."

"Betrayed you?"

Was it Court's imagination, or was Scott genuinely confused. "You were the only one who knew we were going to use Skye as bait at the Viper's Nest."

"I didn't tell anyone," Scott stated in an angry tone. "Who would I tell? Those in the precinct who don't believe? Or the ones who do who would use it against you."

"You were the only one who knew," Court repeated. "You nearly got Skye killed. I didn't realize your hatred of me went so deep."

Court turned and walked to the steps of the porch. He walking through the front door when Scott yelled, "I didn't betray you!"

But Court knew it was a lie, even if he did want to believe him. It always hurt to lose a friend. Yet that was life. People came in and out of your life all the time. Scott was one that was on his way out for good.

CHAPTER NINETEEN

Court laid Skye on the couch and was hit in the back with something that fell to the floor. He glanced behind him to see a pair of jeans.

He put on the jeans. As he was buttoning them, he said, "Y'all can come in now."

"Is it safe?" Riley asked. "Because I don't care to be blinded."

Court chuckled as he put a blanket over Skye. He had no idea how long she would sleep. The situation was over. Hopefully for good. But if he had to, he would fight the vampires and Djinn every day of his life to keep Skye safe.

"I think your brothers want you," Minka said from the doorway.

Court sighed as he stared down at Skye.

Minka came to stand behind him. "I'll stay with

her."

"Thanks," he said and turned on his heel.

Court walked back outside to see his brothers standing naked around Scott, who was arguing with Kane. Court stalked to them.

"Enough!" Court yelled as he reached the group. He glared at Scott. "You had your chance to leave. That's gone now."

Scott returned his scowl with one of his own. "I chose not to leave."

"Then it's your funeral," Kane stated.

Scott shot him a dirty look before his gaze returned to Court. "I didn't betray you."

"You keep saying that, but that doesn't make it true. You're the only one who knew," Court said.

"You expect me to believe that everyone who works for you is to be trusted?"

"Damn straight," Solomon said.

Scott ran a hand down his face. His gaze was beseeching. "Court, man, I didn't do it. As soon as I heard what happened I've been staking out the Viper's Nest. It's how I knew what was going down here."

Court wanted to believe him, but the past was difficult to forget. "You turned your back on me."

"I know." Scott sighed loudly. "I didn't know what to think, and I was young and stupid. That doesn't make what I did right. So many times I wanted to drop by the bar."

Court frowned. "Then why didn't you?"

"Shame. Embarrassment. Worry you might hold a grudge. Take your pick."

Myles crossed his arms over his chest. "It was Scott who reached out to me about a year ago."

"The fact is someone betrayed me," Court said.

"I think I know who it was."

Court whirled around as soon as he heard Skye's voice. He was so glad to see her awake that all he could do was smile. Until her words penetrated his mind. "Who?"

"Helen." Skye walked down the steps and came to stand before Court as she held out jeans for his brothers to take. "I told her what I was going to do."

Kane grunted loudly. "Well, hell."

"That's putting it mildly," Myles replied.

Skye shook her head. "I believe Scott. If he betrayed you, why would he risk his life by being here now?"

"I don't know." Court pulled her against him and held her tight. It felt so good to just hold her.

"You're wounded."

"They'll heal." His heart wouldn't if something had happened to her.

"They better."

He smiled down at her as he ran his hand down her silky length of black hair. Then she pulled away from him and turned them toward Scott.

"Thank you for your help tonight," Skye said. "If you don't mind, I'd like to ask for your help again."

Scott glanced at Court, then nodded. "Name it."

Court looked at Skye, wondering what she was

up to. He didn't want to stand amid the dead vampires and Djinn or talk anymore. He wanted her up in his bed, naked so he could make love to her all night.

"I want you to help me get Helen," Skye announced.

Court blinked. "Skye."

She shook her head and stepped out of his arms, holding up a hand. "Don't, Court. Remember that anger a moment ago when you felt that Scott had betrayed you? Well, that's what I'm feeling. Helen wasn't a friend, but she was my boss and a mentor of sorts. She was the one who urged me to write those articles after I pitched them to her."

"So she put Skye in danger," Kane said.

Court hadn't looked at it that way until that moment. Now he wanted to get his hands on Helen. He reined in his fury – barely.

"How do you want to handle this?" he asked.

Skye smiled and looked around. "With this bunch, it should be easy enough."

"When?"

"No better time than the present."

~ ~ ~

Skye had woken to shouts. Despite Minka trying to keep her lying down, Skye had gone outside to listen. That's when she came to the conclusion that it was Helen who'd betrayed her.

It wasn't nervousness that filled Skye. How could there be any after she'd faced vampires and

Djinn earlier? No, there was only anger and the need for some kind of revenge.

Skye had failed theatre in high school, but this was different. This was her life. And she wanted it back. She had trusted the wrong person, and she'd nearly paid the ultimate price for it.

"Are you sure?" Court asked as they stood in the shadows of the building across the street from the paper's offices.

His concern warmed her heart. She leaned her cheek into the hand he held against her face. "Yes."

"I'd rather go in with you."

"If this is going to work, then you need to remain out here."

"It sucks," he grumbled.

She kissed his palm. "Now you know how I felt earlier. I'll be back soon."

As soon as she tried to turn away, he pulled her back. "Skye, I need to tell you something. I should've told you before the battle."

"What is it?" His anxiousness was worrying her. Was he wanting to end whatever was getting started between them? The mere thought made her clutch the bricks to remain on her feet. She loved him.

He shifted his feet, swallowing loudly. Then he spoke in a rush. "I love you. I know we haven't been together long, but I know what I feel. I don't expect you to return the feeling yet, but I hope you will in time."

Skye threw her arms around his neck. "I love you, too."

"What?" He grew still, his hands barely holding her.

"I love you, too."

There was a moment where he didn't move, didn't utter a sound. And then his arms were around her, holding her so tight she could barely breathe.

His face was buried in her neck. "You've made me the happiest man alive."

Skye laughed as he placed kisses all over her face. Then he suddenly drew back, a frown upon his face. "What is it?"

"Don't go in there," he urged. "Forget Helen."

Skye was shaking her head before he'd finished. "She could do this to someone else, Court. I couldn't live with myself if I allowed that."

"Then let me be with you when you confront her."

Skye was about to refuse him again when she had an idea. She pulled out her cell phone from her pocket and dialed Helen. As soon as her editor picked up the phone Skye put her acting face on. "Oh, Helen, thank God you answered."

"Skye? What's wrong?" her editor asked with just the right amount of concern.

"I'm in trouble. The vampires are after me. I've managed to elude them so far, but I need a place to go."

"Come to the office."

Skye rolled her eyes as Court stood close enough to hear the conversation. "I'm nearly there. Can you take me out of the city?"

"Um...sure. I'll meet you at my car."

Skye ended the call. "I should've thought of that sooner. It's better this way instead of confronting her in her office where there are cameras."

"Come on," Court said as he held out his hand. "Let's get the others and let them know things have changed."

It took only a few minutes to fill Scott and the LaRue brothers in on the new plan as they walked to the parking garage where Helen had her car.

"Are you sure she'll call the vampires?" Scott asked.

Skye shrugged. "We'll find out soon enough."

"I'll hide," Court said. He kissed Skye before he ducked behind a car.

Skye began to pace as if she were nervous and scared. It seemed to take forever for the sound of Helen's heels to be heard on the concrete.

"Skye?"

She came around the back of a tall SUV at the sound of Helen's voice. "Thank you," she said and wiped at her eyes as if she had been crying. "It's been a horrible night."

Helen dug in her purse for her keys. "What happened? Where have you been?"

"Hiding anywhere I could for the last week. That night I went to the Viper's Nest they were expecting me."

Helen's head jerked up. She pushed her graying head of blond hair away from her face. "How?"

"I don't know." Skye hoped she was convincing

enough. It was hard being so close to Helen and not letting the anger take her.

"It's all right. I'll take you somewhere safe."

Skye walked with her, looking over her shoulder as she did. "I need out of New Orleans for awhile."

"Not a problem. I've got some friends that can help."

Skye stopped walking. "The same friends you called to tell I was going back to the club?"

Helen slowed, then stopped. She dropped her arms and turned to face Skye. "When did you figure it out?"

"Not soon enough. Why would you betray me?"

Helen barked in laughter. "Not everything is about you, Skye. You're so focused on what you wanted that you never stopped to think that others might be affected."

"You told me to write the articles!" she yelled.

"Of course. It was a good way to get rid of you."

Skye fisted her hands at her sides. "Why? Why not just tell me the articles wouldn't be of interest?"

"Because you weren't about to give up!" Helen shouted. "You would've gone to anyone who would've listened. Or worse, put them on the Internet yourself. This way, I could regulate what you were saying and take care of you if you got too close."

"Which is what happened with the Djinn," Skye surmised.

Helen shrugged. "Shit happens. You stepped in

the wrong pile. This is my city. These are my people."

"The humans or the supernatural?"

"Both," Helen said with a lift of her chin. "It has taken me years, but I've made connections in both worlds that keep me protected."

There was a sound of male laughter as Scott turned the corner near Helen's car. "That's quite a confession."

"Oh, please," Helen said. "The police will do nothing to me."

"You're probably right," Scott said.

Helen flicked her shoulder-length hair back. "Detective, you'd have been better served staying out of this. Now you'll die with Skye this night."

At that moment, three vampires came out of nowhere. Skye cut her gaze to Helen. "You won't get away with this."

"Of course, I will," Helen said with a laugh. She turned on her heel to go to her car, but drew up short when she caught sight of Court.

Skye smiled at her man. He was glorious in his fury. The three vampires were quickly dispatched by Myles, Solomon, and Kane.

Helen stumbled backward and turned to Skye, beseeching her. "Don't let him hurt me."

"So you know who he is?" Skye asked.

Helen nodded, glancing at Court. "He's a LaRue. They police the factions."

"What do you expect me to do?"

"Mercy," Helen begged as she dropped to her knees.

Skye wanted revenge, but seeing Helen on her knees changed her mind. She looked up at Court. He was waiting on her decision, letting her make the call.

"Leave," Skye said to Helen. "Leave the city and never return."

Helen's face went blank. "But...this is my home."

"You asked for mercy," Court stated in a deep voice. "That's the extent of it. Leave or face the consequences."

Helen nodded and got to her feet. "I'll start packing."

"You have two days," Court said.

Skye walked out of the parking garage with Court. Solomon, Kane, Myles, and Scott were behind them.

"Do you think she'll leave?" Skye asked.

Court shrugged. "I don't know."

"I hope to hell she does," Solomon said.

Myles sighed. "Me, too. I've no wish to carry out Court's threat."

It was the first time Skye had walked down the streets of the city in a week. She looked around noticing the forms in the shadows that watched them.

"Who are they?" she asked in a low voice.

Kane came up beside her. "They're from the other four factions. You'll be left alone now."

"We showed our strength tonight," Myles said.

Court laced his fingers with hers. "It was long overdue."

They walked for another five minutes in silence before Court turned her down a street. Skye saw the others continue.

"Where are we going?" she asked.

Court smiled. "My place."

"Is that right?" She smiled, excitement rushing through her.

"It's where I intend to keep you for quite awhile without any interruptions."

"What about what I want?"

They reached the door to a building and he pushed her against it, crowding her so that their bodies were touching shoulder to hip. "What do you want?" he whispered as he let his mouth draw close to hers before pulling back.

"You. I want you."

His mouth descended on hers in a scorching kiss that had desire pooling in her belly. A moment later, the door opened and they walked inside, still kissing.

EPILOGUE

A month later...

"I can't believe we're at the courthouse," Court said.

Skye stopped him, putting the bouquet of flowers between her arm and body so she could adjust his tie before smoothing her hands down the front of his suit. "It'll be over quickly."

"I only put on this suit for you."

She smiled. "You look very handsome in a suit."

"Come on then," he said and took her hand.

They went up the remainder of the steps and walked through the doors of the courthouse. They found Solomon, Riley, Kane, and Minka standing together.

"Well?" Court asked.

Solomon looked at his watch. "It's time.

They're late."

"No, we're not," Myles said as he and Addison walked up.

Addison was beaming. Skye was thrilled that she and Myles had decided to forgo a long engagement. Neither wanted a big wedding, so they opted to be married by a judge.

Skye walked with the others into the room and awaited the judge. He arrived, and the ceremony was quickly underway. As Skye listened to Myles and Addison exchange vows, all she could think about was her and Court.

She was deliriously happy. After all her hating of the supernatural, she couldn't believe she was dating one. It was actually more than dating. She and Court were all but living together. They had yet to make it official, but they were rarely apart.

They stayed at his place for a few days and then went to hers. Her days were spent at the newspaper, but she was no longer writing articles about the supernatural. She had moved to the advice column.

"What are you thinking about?" Court leaned over and whispered.

She glanced up at him. "You."

"Ah. That's good since I was thinking of you."

"What about?"

"That I love you, and I want us to live together."

"Isn't that what we're doing?" she joked.

He held out his hand. Skye looked down and saw a key. She realized then it was a key to his apartment.

"Move in with me, Skye. Or I'll move in with you. I don't care as long as we're together. I want you with me always."

Skye took the key and held it against her heart with a smile. "Yes, I'll move in with you."

"Be with me? Always?"

Skye waited for the judge to announce that Addison and Myles were husband and wife. Then she turned to Court. "Yes."

They sealed their vows with a kiss.

~ ~ ~

Riley left the courthouse, intending to meet up with Minka. She was halfway to her truck when the hairs on the back of her neck stood on end.

It was the third time in as many days. Riley turned her head and saw the woman across the busy street. She was dressed in all white, which made her dark skin appear even darker. Her black eyes were trained on Riley as she smiled knowingly.

Delphine.

Riley had faced many monsters in her days of hunting, but nothing put the fear in her like the Voodoo priestess. Delphine was letting Riley know she was marked. She would be coming for Riley soon.

With a wave, Delphine turned a corner and disappeared. Riley leaned against her truck as she bent over and tried to figure out what she was going to do about this new situation.

Look for the next story in the Chiasson/LaRue series with **WILD FEVER** – Coming **May 18, 2015**!

Until then, read on for the sneak peek…

Night's off were one of his simple pleasures. Christian blew out a breath as he put his truck in park and got out. He looked at the sign on the building that read Joel's Place.

Normally, he would spend his night off at home, but since the house he shared with his three brothers also had their women, he preferred some time alone.

Christian walked to the bar and opened the door. He was immediately blasted with music and laughter. Stepping inside, he let his gaze wander the place. It might be his night off, but he was a Chiasson, which meant he was always working since the supernatural never took a day off.

He made his way to the bar and ordered a beer as he continued to survey the people. Ghosts, demons, vampires, witches, werewolves. If they preyed on the innocent, then the Chiassons hunted – and killed – them.

His family had been protecting the parish for generations, and thanks to his brothers finding love, that would continue.

Christian's thoughts went to his sister. Riley. She was the one who was supposed to get out of the life. It's why he and his brothers all agreed to send her away to college.

But they should've paid more attention when she called. Riley was a Chiasson to the core. Stubborn, independent, and determined. She was no longer in Austin, Texas. That fact worried Christian as nothing else could. Riley was smart, strong, and beautiful, but she also had a habit of being at the wrong place at the wrong time.

Their family had enemies. Enemies who had already tried to kill them.

"Hey?" Sherriff Marshall Ducet said as he took the seat next to Christian.

Christian nodded in greeting. "You really come here often?"

"Yeah." Marshall looked around and shrugged. "It's a nice place. No...unwanteds here."

Marshall was a transplant from New Orleans. He left the city to get away from the supernatural, only to land smack in the middle of one of the places in North America that they flocked to.

"Plenty of pretty women," Marshall said, wiggling his eyebrows.

Christian glanced at two women shooting pool who kept eyeing him. They were attractive. Either one would do nicely as his bed partner for the night.

Emphasis on *the night*. Unlike Vincent, Lincoln, and Beau, Christian would do whatever it took to ensure he didn't fall in love.

Ever.

"One for each of us," Marshall said.

Christian snorted. "Find your own. Those two

are mine."

"You're a braver man than I if you want to take two women into your bed."

"What's the matter, Marshall? Worried you couldn't please both of them?" Christian asked as he turned his head back to the sheriff.

That's when his gaze was snagged on a vision with pale brown curls that fell past her shoulders. She was wearing a white shirt that showed off her bronze skin, dipping low enough in the front to get a glimpse of cleavage.

Christian leaned to the side to see her faded jeans and cowboy boots. She waved at someone. Christian quickly followed her line of sight and saw one of the bartenders, the female, return the wave.

Curls smiled, her face lighting up as she walked to a barstool and sat at the corner, giving Christian a perfect view of her.

His body responded instantly, causing his balls to tighten in need. Christian brought his beer to his lips and drank deeply as he took in her oval face and large eyes. The dim lighting of the bar prevented him from seeing the exact shade of her eyes however.

With her full lips, delicate jaw, stubborn chin, and slender neck, Curls wasn't just pretty – she was intriguing.

"Ah, I see someone has caught your eye," Marshall said.

Christian pulled his gaze away from the woman. "Just checking things out."

"Right. Adding another to your stable?"

Curls was the kind of woman he would want all to himself. No sharing there. "Yep."

Marshall snorted. "Want to play a game of pool?"

"Sure." Christian took another drink of beer and spun around on the stool to follow Marshall.

Marshall raked the balls while Christian set aside his beer and grabbed a cue stick. It was fate that brought Marshall into their lives, but Christian was glad they had someone they could trust in a seat of power.

Few people of the parish actually knew what the Chiassons did, but there were some that joined in a hunt when needed. Though the majority didn't have a clue that his family had saved their hides on multiple occasions, they seemed to realize the Chiassons were dangerous.

Dangerous didn't even begin to cover what they were. What kind of man brought a woman into such a family and the constant threat of death? His brothers might be willing to do it, but not him.

He remembered all too well his mother's murder and his father's death that night all those years ago. It was enough to ensure that Christian remained alone. There was little time to protect everyone. Why would he add a wife and children into the mix?

Only an idiot would do that.

His brothers, obviously, were idiots.

Thank you for reading **Moon Thrall**. I hope you enjoyed it! If you liked this book – or any of my other releases – please consider rating the book at the online retailer of your choice. Your ratings and reviews help other readers find new favorites, and of course there is no better or more appreciated support for an author than word of mouth recommendations from happy readers. Thanks again for your interest in my books!

Donna Grant

www.DonnaGrant.com

Want to stay informed of new releases and special subscriber-only exclusive content?

Be sure to visit

www.DonnaGrant.com

and sign up for Donna's private email newsletter!

ABOUT THE AUTHOR

New York Times and *USA Today* bestselling author Donna Grant has been praised for her "totally addictive" and "unique and sensual" stories. She's written more than thirty novels spanning multiple genres of romance including the bestselling Dark King series featuring immortal Highlander shape shifting dragons who are daring, untamed, and seductive. She lives with her husband, two children, a dog, and four cats in Texas.

Connect online at:

www.DonnaGrant.com

www.facebook.com/AuthorDonnaGrant

www.twitter.com/donna_grant

www.goodreads.com/donna_grant/